ANDRE DEUTSCH

ODDBOD & TIMMY

To my wife, Mary,
great friend, Nobby,
and all my family.
And for Max the Dachs.

My special thanks are due to Vic Lore who suggested
writing something in the first place, to the late Eric
Thompson for his encouragement, and without whose
input Timmy would not be the dog he is, to Angus,
Kieron and Hannah and to Pamela Royds for her tireless
and meticulous editorial guidance.

First published in 1990 by
André Deutsch Limited
105-106 Great Russell Street, London WC1B 3LJ

ISBN 0 233 98529 8

Printed in Great Britain by
WBC Bridgend

BUCKINGHAM PALACE

I first came across Odd Bod and Timmy soon
fter the stories were read at the Blueboys School, in
nchinhampton. My son Peter and I very much enjoyed them.

Now that a book of them is to be
ablished, it is gratifying to know that some of the proceeds from
le sale of this copy will go to The Save the Children Fund.

While young and old are enjoying the
ompany of Odd Bod and Timmy, you will be giving valuable support
o work that may well include basic education for children who
ight not otherwise receive any and therefore not be able to enjoy
ld Bod and Timmy or any other book.

Anne

ONTENTS

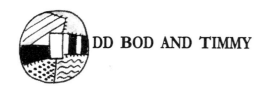

ODD BOD AND TIMMY

There was nobody quite as odd as Odd Bod.

Everything about him was odd. His house was odd. His dog was odd. He was most odd. Indeed there were people who thought he was a very funny man. And he was. Quite extraordinary. Not only did he look unusual, but he behaved in a way that could hardly be called conventional.

For a start, he wore a rather old-fashioned long red coat, a yellow shirt, patchwork trousers and always odd socks. He had two eyes, a nose, a mouth, of course he did, like most of us, but they didn't seem to be put together in quite the right way. His fingers were too podgy. His legs were too long. He had a head that was a size too large, an over-pointed nose and not really enough hair.

No, there was nobody quite as strange as Odd Bod. Above all else, however, he was a very kind man. Very sensitive, but also extremely shy. When he was doing one thing, he was always thinking about doing something else, which didn't make things easier for him. In fact for Odd Bod, life was exceptionally difficult.

His house was quite small. It was a cottage, really, but it had an enormous garden. You should have seen it. A real picture. Just about every kind of flower grew there, and Odd Bod used to go around talking to the plants, helping them to grow. He loved his garden and it showed.

It showed in the grass that was always well cut. It showed in the pathways that were always cared for. It showed in the way he tied up his tall flowers, always saw that they had enough water in the summer, always made sure they had enough room to breathe.

Yes, Odd Bod certainly was a very kind man. He was so kind in fact that he would always pick a worm up from the pavement if it had come out in the rain and put it back in the garden, where it was safe from treading feet.

Odd Bod's house was at the end of a lane. He had one great friend, Timmy. Timmy was a large black dog, who lived with him. The two were devoted to each other; well, Timmy was in his own peculiar way and, as dogs and people often do, they had grown to look somewhat like each other.

Timmy was highly critical of a lot that Odd Bod did, usually without reason, of course. For instance, he felt that Odd Bod made far too much of his flowers. Their importance, to his mind at least, was exaggerated beyond belief. The time Odd Bod spent fussing over them could, in Timmy's opinion, be put to far better use fussing over Timmy.

Timmy's habits were inclined to be a trifle erratic. He would bark at invisible visitors, chase imaginary cats or suddenly start wagging his tail for no apparent reason. None of this seemed to bother Odd Bod, except when Timmy barked too loudly. He accepted the dog for what he was and loved him more than anything else in the world. There were times when Odd Bod lost his patience and shouted at Timmy if his behaviour passed the bounds of what even Odd Bod would accept. That didn't happen very often and it certainly didn't last for long if it did.

Timmy, on the other hand, was given to quite considerable and prolonged bouts of sulking if things didn't go quite his way. He always slept downstairs in a bed that Odd Bod had made specially for him, and seemed to know all that Odd Bod said to him, although sometimes he chose not to understand.

There were occasions when Timmy proved himself to be exceptionally clever. He was able to transfer messages into Odd Bod's mind, but could never quite work out when, let alone how. It wasn't easy, and there were times when Timmy found that his powers seemed to let him down very badly. Timmy could also be rather selfish. What he wanted to do, where he wanted to be, always came first.

For example, if he wanted to stretch out in a particular patch of sunlight, he wouldn't bother to check first to see whether there were any flowers there. If there were, they were squashed. It was their bad luck for being in his way. Odd Bod found this extremely hard to accept.

The two went everywhere together, except when Timmy was overtaken by a fit of the most incredible laziness. On these occasions he wouldn't stir from his basket and Odd Bod knew better than to try to persuade him.

One day Odd Bod had a real shock. It was one that he didn't get over for a long while. When it was time for Timmy's dinner, Odd Bod called him, but there was no sign of him anywhere. This was unheard of. Timmy had one great passion above all else: food. He ate, slept and drank it, you could say. Odd Bod was puzzled. As far as he could remember, Timmy had never done such a thing before. He was always within earshot in case he missed anything. Odd Bod called and called, but Timmy chose not to appear.

Finally, he decided to go and look for Timmy. He took his hat and coat and walking stick and started out towards the centre of the village. Odd Bod kept calling Timmy's name. First of all quite gently, 'Timmy, Timmy. Where are you, boy? Your supper's out.' Then, as he became more worried, his voice took on a harder note. 'Timmy. Timmy. Where the devil are you? Just wait until I find you. I'll teach you a lesson you won't forget.'

He spoke like that only because he was anxious and not able to find the dog. Odd Bod continued calling Timmy's name. People stared at him as he went by, but nobody stopped to ask if they could do anything. Odd Bod became sadder and sadder. He began to think that he would never see Timmy again. 'I'll kill that dog,' he thought to himself. 'Going off like that. Without leaving a note.' He stopped short in his tracks. 'Whatever am I saying? I've never killed anything in my life, except weeds. Even the flies go free when I'm around, so I certainly wouldn't think of killing Timmy.'

Odd Bod came to an oak tree near the village pond. He sat down to try to work out what to do. Where *could* Timmy have gone? What could have happened to him? The more Odd Bod thought about it, the worse it became. He started to imagine all sorts of things. Maybe Timmy had fallen down a well. Perhaps he had been run over. What if somebody had taken him off somewhere? Anything could happen these days. Odd Bod was always reading in his newspaper about people going missing, but he would not have dreamed that it might happen to Timmy.

He thought that he would go into the village shop and ask if anyone had seen him. This seemed to be the most likely place; the shop was the centre of things, as far as the village was concerned. It took a lot of courage for Odd Bod to do this because he wasn't used to talking to other people. He found talking to himself rather better. The answers he received seemed much more reliable than the ones other people gave him.

This time, however, it was different. Timmy could be in trouble. Odd Bod forgot about his shyness and stood up to go. As he did so, he caught his coat on a small stump. There was a splitting sound. 'Bother,' said Odd Bod. 'Oh well, I can't worry about that now. I've more important things on my mind.'

The bell tinkled loudly as he walked through the door of the shop. The people inside stopped their gossip and stared as Odd Bod came in. He didn't care. All he minded about was Timmy. And he wanted him back, with all his

faults, so that every-
thing could be as it had
been before. Odd Bod
went up to the counter.
'Excuse me,' he said to
the assistant, who was
wrapping up bacon, 'have you
seen my black dog anywhere? He
went out for a walk by himself
and I've lost him.'

'No, I'm afraid not,' said the
lady. 'I do hope you find him.'
She spoke softly and had a very
kind face. Odd Bod thanked
her and walked slowly out
of the shop. As he did so,
his coat caught on a display
of canned beans. They came
tumbling down.

'Oh dear me. Now look what I've done,' he said,
more confused than ever, starting to put the cans back.

'Never mind,' said the lady. 'It doesn't matter. I'll
see to them. It's more important that you find your
dog.'

Odd Bod left the shop and started to make his way

back home, feeling more lonely than he had ever done before. He passed all the places where he and Timmy had gone for walks, remembering all the fun they had had together.

He did love that dog. Odd Bod thought of Timmy's enormous appetite and how much he liked his buttered turnips. 'That's what I can't understand. He hadn't had his dinner. I wish I hadn't talked of killing him now. He may be dead for all I know.' There never would be another dog like Timmy. Odd Bod was quite sure of that. He couldn't remember ever having lost anything so precious. 'I'll never find another friend like him,' he thought. 'It's my fault for not taking more care.'

The nearer home he came, the slower Odd Bod walked. He didn't want to go back to the empty cottage. He simply couldn't face it. Just then he thought he heard the sound of Timmy's name disc chinking on his collar. He turned round full of joy, expecting to see the dog ambling up as if nothing had happened, but the lane was empty. There was nothing. No one in sight.

'I must just get used to the fact that he's gone,' Odd Bod said to himself, but it didn't make him feel any better. He came to his gate, pushed it open and went through the front door, which was ajar. Then, surprise, surprise, who should be there, lying in his basket, fast asleep, but Timmy.

Odd Bod was beside himself with joy. He didn't even ask Timmy where he'd been. Instead, he brought him his favourite bone and put it in his basket for when he woke up.

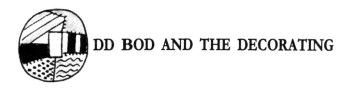 DD BOD AND THE DECORATING

When Timmy woke up, it was the next morning. Odd Bod was in the kitchen, looking at the wall. 'Gracious me, the paint is beginning to peel off,' he said to Timmy. 'We can't have that.'

The fact that the paint had been peeling off for the past year was beside the point. This was the first time Odd Bod had actually noticed it. He may have been the kindest of men, but he wasn't the most observant.

Things like peeling paint didn't really bother him, not for long at any rate. He would go on, day in, day out, not noticing, then all of a sudden he would see it and that would be that. Something would have to be done immediately. Odd Bod was a man of instant action, in some things at least. If he didn't want to do a thing, however, he would sit in his rocking chair for hours at a stretch, thinking of reasons why he shouldn't do it.

'I can't seem to get going today,' he would say to Timmy. Timmy understood perfectly. He had the same trouble. He'd always fancied being a racing greyhound, but couldn't seem to get the hang of it. To go back to the peeling paint, however, once Odd Bod had spotted it, that was it. 'Action stations!' he yelled at Timmy. 'It's got to be done, boy.'

Timmy sniffed. You could say a lot with a sniff, he always thought. Timmy could remember the last time Odd Bod had tried his hand at decorating. What a mess there'd been – paint everywhere and every-thing upside down. Timmy was not looking forward to a second time round at all. He simply could not see the point.

'First of all I'll move everything upstairs, then I'll go and buy some wallpaper. No, first of all I'll buy the paper, then we'll do the moving,' said Odd Bod, having second thoughts and working everything out extremely quickly. 'You stay there, boy. I won't be long,' he continued to the bemused Timmy.

'That's a bit of luck,' thought the dog. 'If he's going shopping, I'll have an hour or so's peace. With a bit of luck, that is. I'd better cross my paws, I suppose. You can't be too careful in these matters.'

Odd Bod set off for the village. He knew exactly the sort of paper he wanted. Purple stripes with pink spots. 'We have this one,' said the man. 'It's pretty close.' The paper was pale blue, with roses climbing all over it.

'Is it?' replied Odd Bod doubtfully. 'I suppose so. Well, I like roses. Yes, that will do very nicely, thank you. I'll have six rolls, please. And some paste.' The man behind the counter wrapped up the paper and paste. Odd Bod paid him and went back home. It took him rather longer than he had expected, because the paper kept slipping from under his arm, and Odd Bod had to stop every few steps to recover the rolls. 'Timmy will like this,' he thought, cheering himself up as he walked along.

'There, Timmy, what do you think of that?' Odd Bod asked the dog. Timmy opened one eye. 'Not more flowers,' he thought. 'I can't bear it. I have enough trouble with the ones in the garden.'

Odd Bod didn't even stop for a cup of tea. 'We'll have this done in no time at all,' he said to the dog, thinking he might possibly get him interested. Timmy, bored with the day so far, decided to send out one of his messages. 'I like my eggs well done, with crispy bits round the outside,' he signalled, very slowly and deliberately, in case Odd Bod's mind happened to be elsewhere.

Odd Bod went on with his work and carried everything, except the table, upstairs. He would need that for pasting the paper. Timmy's signal apparently went wide of target. 'I don't go much on this telepathic lark,' thought the dog. 'It only works to suit itself.'

'I'll put your basket out in the sun,' said Odd Bod. Timmy perked up. Life was definitely getting better. 'With a bit more luck, it could be bacon for tea,' he thought, pushing it a bit. 'I wonder what my stars say.'

Odd Bod took off his red coat and put on white overalls. Then he cleaned the paintwork and started to rub the walls down. 'No need to waste too much time on these,' he said to himself. 'I'll only cover them up with the paper. Perhaps we could have some music, while we're about it.' Odd Bod switched on the radio. A jumble of sound roared out. It was so loud, he almost dropped the scrubbing brush. 'Maybe not,' he said and switched it off again. 'Sounds a bit too progressive for me. I like something a bit more soothing when I'm working.'

Outside, Timmy was making the most of his sunbathing. 'He's not such a bad stick, I suppose,' he thought, graciously. 'I could do worse. So could he, of course. I could be a proper little tearaway, messing the place up all day. These things work both ways, you see.' Timmy was often given to reviewing his good points. He didn't spend too much time on the bad ones, believing firmly in the power of positive thinking.

Odd Bod fetched his step ladder in order to reach the ceiling. Somehow, however, he forgot to take the bucket of water up with him. Then, as he was coming down from the steps, he forgot that he had left the bucket where it was. His foot went straight into the dirty water. 'There's a thing,' he said. 'Now I'll have to change my socks.' It took him quite a while to search out another odd pair. Finally, he found them and started work again. This time everything was all right, and he finished cleaning the ceiling.

Odd Bod opened a can of paint and went to find a brush. Timmy came in and accidentally knocked over the paint pot. Odd Bod returned. 'Oh, Timmy, now look what you've done,' said Odd Bod. 'Never mind, you didn't mean to, and it won't take long to clear up.' Timmy returned to his basket, out of harm's way.

'Some tea would be nice,' he thought. 'And a biscuit, perhaps. Nothing too fancy. One of those with cream in the middle would be very acceptable. Another thing . . . I wonder what I would have been like at algebra. Brilliant, I should imagine, if I'd ever been taught it,' Timmy pondered, his thoughts jumping from one thing to another, as usual.

Odd Bod cleared up the mess and started painting. The paint had been left over from last time. Odd Bod was not a man to throw anything away, if he could possibly avoid it. By lunch-time, he had finished everything – doors, windows and ceiling. Odd Bod was a very rapid worker, once he got going. 'I think I'll work through lunch,' he said to Timmy. 'We'll eat this evening.'

Timmy looked, disapprovingly, but accepted the inevitable. 'Another one of his fast days, I suppose,' he thought to himself. 'They always seem to go so slowly to me.'

Odd Bod started on the papering. He measured and cut and pasted and waited. Then it was time to hang the first piece. He chose a suitable spot, hung the paper and brushed it out. Unfortunately he had forgotten to take down grandfather's plate, which bulged rather badly. Odd Bod sighed, lifted the paper and removed the plate. 'I don't think I'll put it back,' he said to himself. 'In case it happens again the next time I decorate.' Odd Bod smoothed the paper down and stood back to admire his work. 'I'll have this done in no time at all,' he said.

Timmy came in from the garden again. For one delicious second he could have sworn he smelled buttered turnips. His normally slow-moving eyes leaped into action. Checked. Swivelled. Recorded. Negative. Unfortunately, a piece of paper was hanging, pasted side out, from the table. Timmy somehow touched it. It wound instantly round his head. He was suddenly covered in roses. 'Oh, Timmy, I told you to stay in your basket,' said Odd Bod. Timmy stomped off, trailing a length of paper behind him.

Odd Bod went on papering. By tea-time, he had nearly finished. There was just one more piece to go. It was finally in position. Timmy came in again. Were

they ever going to eat? He had never known Odd Bod
to be so carried away with anything. The kitchen really
did look very good. Odd Bod was most surprised. He
had changed his mind about the plate and it beamed
once more from its usual position. 'I'm not too sure
about the roses. What do you think, Timmy?'

Timmy thought he could smell soup. Was it tomato?
No. Onion, laced with spiced walnuts and a
touch of thyme? No. Turnip with a hint of
vindaloo and mulberry jelly? No. 'Dreaming
as usual,' he thought. 'Still, one day, when
I'm rich and famous . . . Now what was he
saying . . . something about thinking, wasn't
it? Or was it drinking? Yes, I could just do
with a nice bowl of milk. Which reminds
me, where did I put my bone?'

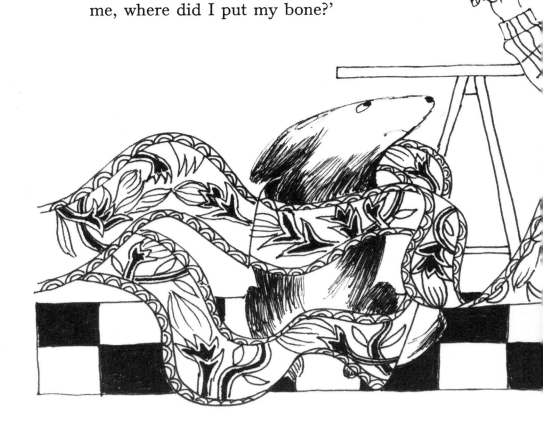

Timmy, whose mind, when it was working in top gear, did so in a most baffling way, trotted out into the garden and sniffed the pale blue air. 'Some stupid fool's hidden it,' he thought. 'Why does life have to be so unbelievably complicated? I'm sure I left it under the blackberry bush. I must be getting old or something.' He stopped short. 'Now then, Timmy,' he reprimanded himself, 'don't let's get morbid. That's quite enough of that,' and he made off

in the general direction of the mulberry tree. He didn't believe in going directly anywhere. It always made the arrival so much more of a discovery.

He made it, finally, and rummaged around in the bushes, his nose tuned to the frequency of the lost treasure. Timmy came across an old sock. 'So that's where you got to,' he thought. 'I wondered where I'd left you. I've been looking for you for days.'

'Timmy!' Odd Bod called from the doorway.

'Now what?' wondered Timmy.

'Timmy,' came the voice again. 'Tea.'

'That's different,' Timmy thought.

'Oh there you are,' said Odd Bod, putting down Timmy's food. Timmy savoured the moment, approached the bowl with as much dignity as he could muster and then, when he could contain himself no longer, woofed right in.

'Slowly, slowly!' squeaked Odd Bod. 'You haven't got a train to catch.'

'Here we go again,' thought Timmy. 'Same old ritual. Just when I was enjoying myself. What have trains to do with turnips anyway? He does talk some awful rubbish sometimes. In any case, when did I last go on a train? It must be years since we had a holiday.'

'I think it's time we had a holiday,' said Odd Bod. 'I must fix up something. Somewhere sunny for a change.'

'Good gracious. It works. I must be telepathic after all,' thought Timmy. 'As well as everything else. I must try this more often.' He chomped through the last juicy morsel. 'Yes, much more often.'

'So Timmy, what do you think of my roses?' asked Odd Bod. Timmy yawned. The day had all been just a bit too much.

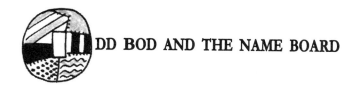# ODD BOD AND THE NAME BOARD

Odd Bod thought that it was time his cottage had a name. It hadn't had one since he bought it, and that was years ago. He sat down in his rocking chair to think about it. 'We could call it Odd Bod's,' he thought. This was not, however, very fair on Timmy. Not only that, it would have to have the word 'cottage' in the title . . .

Odd Bod thought some more. Myrtle Cottage. That sounded nice. Myrtle Cottage. He would have to have some notepaper printed, which was no problem. He had a small printing press of his own. Myrtle Cottage. Yes, that wasn't bad. 'Myrtle Cottage. What do you think of that, Timmy?' Odd Bod asked the dog. Timmy was asleep. He opened one eye wearily. 'I've thought of the name – Myrtle Cottage. What do you think of it?' repeated Odd Bod. Timmy sniffed. He was never at his best early in the morning and was in no shape to think about anything. He closed his eye, hoping that Odd Bod would get the message.

'I see,' said Odd Bod. 'It was just a thought.' Odd Bod rarely did anything without asking Timmy first. He was a very wise dog and Odd Bod found him useful for trying out his ideas. 'Yes, I see,' said Odd Bod. 'Not all that happy with that one, are we?' Timmy shifted a leg. His powers of telepathy were clearly not what he'd hoped they'd be. Sleep was what was required at the moment. Sleep. Could the man not understand that?

Odd Bod went outside to have a look at the cottage. He walked right round it, pad in hand, trying to get the feel of it. 'I'll jot down what happens to mind,' he said. 'You never know. Something may come of it.' Odd Bod put his forefinger to his forehead in an attempt to aid thought. 'How about Pear Tree Cottage? That sounds rather good.'

The fact that there was no pear tree in sight did not bother him over much. Odd Bod was not a man to be too fussy about details. Details were boring things and he seldom let them get in his way. 'Yes, Pear Tree Cottage, I like that,' he smiled. 'Let's put that down, at least for starters.' Odd Bod went on strolling round the cottage. 'Well Cottage. That's another one,' he said suddenly. Again, there was no well. This did not seem to matter either. He wrote it down. Well Cottage. Then it dawned on Odd Bod. 'No well,' he said to himself. 'We can't have that.' He crossed the name out. 'Could call it Christmas Cottage, I suppose. No, perhaps not.'

'That leaves Pear Tree Cottage – that's still favourite, but again there's no pear tree. If I go on like this, I'll never get anywhere. There are so many things I haven't got, I'll never get a name. I could just call it The Cottage, I suppose.' Odd Bod wrote it down. 'It's not very original,' he said. 'What about The Cottage?' Odd Bod called in to Timmy. There was silence, apart from a very brief snore. 'Hm,' said Odd Bod. 'I see what you mean.'

Odd Bod stopped to pick a daisy from the lawn. He twiggled it around in his fingers. Daisy Cottage he wrote down. He crossed it out. 'Sounds a bit fancy,' he said. 'Timmy wouldn't like that much. No. Pear Tree Cottage is the best so far. Perhaps I like it so much because there *is* no pear tree. I mean, if there were one, it wouldn't be very original. No, Pear Tree Cottage it is. On all counts.'

He went inside. 'Pear Tree Cottage,' Odd Bod said to the still slumbering Timmy. 'Pear Tree Cottage, boy,' Odd Bod repeated, right in Timmy's ear. Timmy woke up and wagged his tail.

'Thank goodness that's over,' thought the dog. 'No chance of anything to eat, I suppose? Silly question. As if there ever is. If only I could reach the cooker, I'd show him a thing or two. I'm sure my mother was a Gordon Blue.'

'Now I'll have to make a name board,' said Odd Bod.

'This I have to see,' thought Timmy, who could not now get back to sleep. 'He's bound to make a mess of it.' Timmy stepped out of his basket. 'I mean, it's all right if you have the talent for that kind of thing. I'd probably be all right, you see, but I think he should stick to what he's

good at – gardening, for instance, a useless pastime, but if he likes it – and cooking something for me, of course. He's quite good at that. Sometimes. Talking of which, is that an apple fritter on the floor? No, a trick of the light, as usual,' he thought, and stomped off into the garden to worry the flowers.

Odd Bod was not really very good with his hands. The practical side, apart from his garden, did tend to give him problems, but at least he tried. First, he found a suitable piece of wood and some nails. Then he started knocking the nails into the wood to make up the word 'Pear'.

'Ah that's a thought,' he said to himself. 'I could have called it Horseshoe Cottage. It's a bit late, though, to think of changing it at this stage. No, we'd better stick to the name we have . . . I suppose I could make the sign

read "Horseshoe Cottage, formerly Pear Tree Cottage", but then I'd need a bigger board,' Odd Bod went on. 'Come on, you're being stupid. In any case, it's nearly tea time.' Timmy perked up at the best words he'd heard all day. Odd Bod went on hammering. He had just got to the 'e' in 'Cottage' when he ran out of nails.

'There's a thing,' said Odd Bod. 'Now I'll have to go to the village. I hope the shop will still be open.' He went inside and looked at the time. It was five o'clock. 'I'll have to hurry,' he said. 'Coming boy?' Odd Bod asked Timmy. The dog ambled out of his basket, not exactly full of joy at the idea. 'I do believe I could have been a homing pigeon if I'd put my mind to it,' he thought.

Odd Bod reached the village shop only to find that it was early closing day. 'Closed 1 pm on Wednesdays' the sign said. 'Bother,' thought Odd Bod. 'I'd completely forgotten.' Life did seem to have its problems. 'We'll just have to come back tomorrow.'

'I'm not so sure about the "we",' thought Timmy.

The next day, Odd Bod set off on his own. No surprise, Timmy decided to stay at home. He bought the nails and returned to the cottage. Odd Bod finished off the board and held it up. You could, if you were very clever, read 'Pear Tree Cottage'. 'Now that's what I call artistic,' said Odd Bod and hung the sign over his front door.

'Or catastrophic, even,' thought Timmy. 'I wonder where he put my bone. If only he'd concentrate on my diet a bit more. I'm sure I'm underweight for my length. Or is it height? Both, I shouldn't wonder, but it doesn't seem to bother him. One day I won't be here, and then he'll be sorry.' Timmy started off on one of his melancholic meanderings, all oozing self-pity. Nobody loved him. Nobody wanted him. Nobody cared.

'Come to think of it, a pear tree would look rather nice there.' Odd Bod broke into Timmy's fit of gloom. 'I think I'll go and buy one after all. What do you think, Tim?'

Timmy wagged his tail. 'Did somebody mention trees?' That's one thing he was in favour of. Any day. Yes. Definitely. Trees. You could bury bones under trees and sleep in their shade on hot days. And trees didn't make you go for long, boring walks.

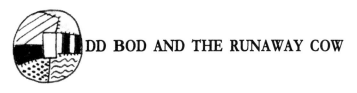

ODD BOD AND THE RUNAWAY COW

Odd Bod was all ready for the village Flower Festival. He had a row of very special flowers which were coming into bloom just in time for it. Every day, Odd Bod went out and fussed over them. He talked to them, too, as he did to all his plants and flowers.

Timmy thought Odd Bod made far too much of them. After all, they were only flowers. And flowers couldn't bark or hunt or gnaw bones. In fact, flowers couldn't do any of the worthwhile things in life that he could. Pretty dull existence really, Timmy used to think, just sitting there all day, doing nothing. What's more, flowers couldn't fry eggs, crispy round the outside, as Timmy liked them.

Timmy could think what he liked, however, Odd Bod was absolutely devoted to his flowers. He spent a great deal of time in his garden and certainly had something to show for all his hard work. It was probably the most beautiful garden you could ever hope to find.

Right now, Odd Bod's mind was firmly on the Festival. Last year, he had narrowly missed First Prize. This year he hoped that he would be luckier. His garden and Timmy were really what he lived for. Timmy did not always appreciate this, though.

When he finished working, Odd Bod always cleaned his tools thoroughly and put them away in the garden shed. He was a very precise man. Everything had a special place and had to be put exactly where it belonged. That was the way to keep some sort of order in your life, he decided. Timmy couldn't understand this at all. He thought that it was much more fun trying to guess where

things were and coming across them unexpectedly.

That evening Odd Bod took Timmy for a stroll to the village green and back. If Timmy could wriggle out of going for a walk, he would, but there was no chance this time. Odd Bod insisted because it was such a beautiful evening. Once they were home, Odd Bod went out into the garden to take one last look at his flowers. 'If he looks at those flowers once more,' thought Timmy, 'I shall scream. Well perhaps not. It might upset my general level headedness. Anyway, my voice has broken once. I don't want to break it again.'

The next day was the day of the Festival. Odd Bod was very excited. He went to bed, but couldn't sleep. He read for a while, then finally put out the light and dozed off. When he woke up, it was daylight. He washed and dressed and went downstairs into the kitchen to make his morning cup of tea.

First of all he drew the kitchen curtains as he always did, the kettle in one hand waiting to be filled. To Odd Bod's great surprise, two large brown eyes were staring in at him. He was so taken aback, he nearly dropped the kettle. 'That must be Farmer Wilkes' cow, Daphne,' Odd Bod thought to himself. 'How can she have got in? She must have broken down the fence.'

Odd Bod went outside to talk to Daphne. Of all animals, apart from Timmy of course, cows were his favourites. He loved their huge eyes and the gentle way they looked at you. When Odd Bod saw what had happened, however, he was not so sure he liked them after all. Daphne had been right along his prize row of flowers

25

and eaten all the heads off. She had ignored everything else in the garden, but had gone straight for the things that mattered most.

'Daphne, how could you have done such a thing?' Odd Bod asked the cow, who still had the remains of one prize bloom hanging from her mouth.

'Moo,' said Daphne, shedding the petals as she opened her mouth.

Odd Bod chased her out of the garden, through the fence she had broken down and back into the field where she belonged. Just then, Farmer Wilkes appeared. 'Look what Daphne has done,' wailed Odd Bod. 'My prize flowers all ready for the Show and she has eaten the lot.'

'For a second I could have sworn I smelled buttered turnips,' thought Timmy, whose optimism knew no bounds. 'It must have been those chewed up flowers, I suppose.' He had managed to get up more quickly than usual and, feeling that something was afoot, had trotted outside to sniff the morning air. He was at his happiest if disaster was in the offing and he could sense it a mile off. The sight of the cow, with a flower still hanging from her mouth, meant that he was off the hook, for a while, at least. 'I see I was wrong about the turnips. Will I never learn? And when did I last have a bone, answer me that.'

'My word, I am sorry,' said Farmer Wilkes. 'She's never done such a thing before. Did you leave the gate open?'

'No,' said Odd Bod. 'She broke the fence. Look, there's the gap where she came through.'

'It's funny though,' the farmer went on. 'I could have understood it if it had been Deidre, but Daphne doesn't usually wander. I am very sorry.'

'It's not your fault,' said Odd Bod, 'but I did so much want to win the prize this year. It can't be helped, though. Moaning won't bring the flowers back. I'll have to wait until next time.' Odd Bod went inside the house, followed by Timmy, who was completely unmoved by the tragedy. Odd Bod gave the dog his usual morning milk and made himself some tea.

Timmy approached his bowl with a certain lack of interest. 'If you ask me,' he thought, 'there's far too much attention paid to fripperies and not nearly enough care taken over basic essentials. Food for instance. Take this milk – it looks exactly the same as the milk I had yesterday and the day before. If he really thought about it, he could colour it – pink, orange, green and so on – and give me a different colour every day. I always thought variety was meant to be the spice of life. If mine's anything to go by, it's in danger of becoming exceptionally dull. It doesn't take much, when all's said and done. Oh well, I suppose I had better drink it as it is, otherwise he'll get in a state and think I'm sickening for something.'

Presently it was time for the Festival. Odd Bod had recovered from his initial disappointment and was looking forward to seeing other people's flowers. He walked around, admiring all the blooms on show. There were large ones, short ones, tall ones, small ones – all the kinds you could possibly imagine. Soon Odd Bod forgot about his own flowers.

Timmy thought that it was the most incredibly boring afternoon he had ever spent. He could not imagine what other people saw in it all. Eventually, the prizes were given out and then it was time to go home.

'There might be a chance, agreed an outside chance, that there could be crispy pancakes for tea,' thought Timmy. 'If the sun is shining and the gate open when we get home, there will be,' he decided, embarking upon one of his elaborate, superstitious calculations. By the time they reached the cottage, it had started to rain. The gate was tight shut.

'What did I tell you? Just my luck,' thought the dog. 'Just my luck.'

Odd Bod, on the other hand, had his second surprise of the day. Farmer Wilkes had certainly been busy while they were at the Festival. All around the garden was a brand new fence. 'What a kind man he is,' exclaimed Odd Bod. 'He really must have been very sorry for what Daphne did. It only goes to show – I may not have won any prizes at the Festival, but I've a prize fence instead. Come on, Timmy. We must go and thank Farmer Wilkes straight away.'

'Oh really? There's that word again. Must . . . If I must . . . Look at that, he's got me at it now. Can't think what I've got to thank Wilkes for. Wait a minute, though . . . he has plenty of turnips. Maybe . . . No . . . I shouldn't think so. I shouldn't think he puts butter on them, not for a second.'

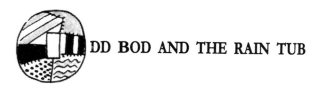 DD BOD AND THE RAIN TUB

It was Thursday, two weeks after Odd Bod had finished the decorating, and it was raining very hard. Odd Bod was standing in his porch, looking out. Timmy was in his usual place when it was raining, curled up in his bed, his nose on the edge of the basket and one eye on the weather outside.

There was no sense in getting up at all really. The dog did not believe in too much exercise even on fine days, but when the weather was like this, facing the day seemed completely pointless. Timmy lay there, deep in thought.

'The only good thing about the rain is that I don't have to go for one of those long walks of his. This means that usually, *usually* that is, not necessarily, of course, but usually, I get something nice to eat. Although if the last three days are anything to go by, I shall be rather unlucky,' he rambled on.

This was the fourth day it had been raining and Odd Bod was bored with it. He liked it when the sun shone, when everything sparkled in the bright light, when the birds sang because they were happy. Rain made Odd Bod sad.

Today was like all the others when it was raining. Odd Bod slopped about in the garden and couldn't get on with anything. He stood there looking particularly glum, because there was something that was worrying him. There was a water butt at the side of his cottage and it was getting very full. Very full indeed. If it rained much more, the butt was bound to overflow. Odd Bod really didn't know what to do to stop it.

He went inside and sat down on his favourite rocking chair next to Timmy. 'Well, Timmy, I don't know what to do,' he said. 'I know what I should have done – something to make the butt stand upright, instead of being on the tilt all the time. If it goes on raining like this, the tub will overflow and all the water will pour into the house.'

Timmy cocked an ear and wagged his tail. It was his answer to most things that Odd Bod said. 'Would I be right in assuming that what is required is a larger butt?' pondered Timmy, pompously. 'It seems pretty simple to me, but then I'm only a dog.'

He stood up in his basket and went over to where Odd Bod was sitting. Timmy put a paw on Odd Bod's knee. He was given to this way of fawning and begging for favours every now and again. It could pay dividends Odd Bod patted Timmy's head. He rocked backwards and forwards in his chair. It was what he always did when he had a problem on his mind. He found it helped him plan things out. It made him feel calm. Timmy's head went backwards and forwards with the movement of the chair, which made him feel quite dizzy.

TIMMY

Odd Bod didn't like to rush things. He preferred to take time to think, see what to do, work it all out. He stopped rocking, went to the door again and looked at the weather. Timmy's head calmed down considerably. It was still raining hard. Odd Bod took his umbrella, put on his rubber boots and went out to have another look at the water butt.

'Now where's he going?' wondered Timmy. 'I should

say a day like today called for soup. Something hot and spicy to take one's mind off the weather, not a walk in the rain.'

The water was about an inch from the top. Timmy looked out of the window. Odd Bod looked up at the sky. It was black, very black indeed. 'There's plenty more to come,' Odd Bod thought to himself. 'I really must do something. It's no good just waiting for the worst to happen.'

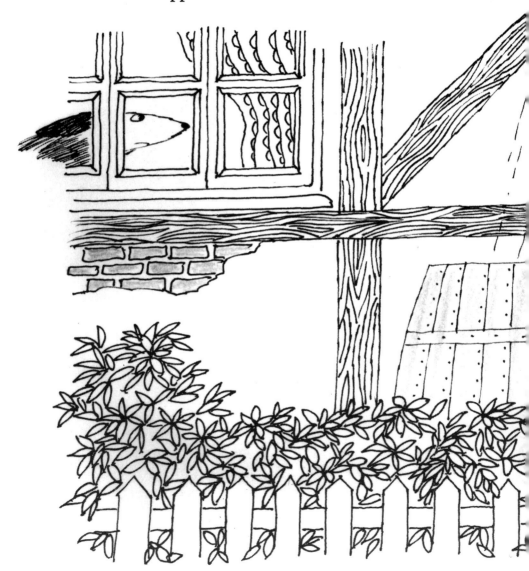

Odd Bod went indoors and left his boots and umbrella by the door. Timmy was back in his basket, curled up very comfortably. His ear dropped when he saw Odd Bod. 'Well, Tim,' said Odd Bod, 'I've thought what's best to do. We must take all our things and put them upstairs, in case the water comes in.' Timmy wagged his tail, but didn't move. Soup was evidently off. His luck was definitely not in. Any possibility of something to eat was clearly out of the question.

'Come on, boy,' said Odd Bod. 'You're first. We'll take your basket upstairs, so you'll be all right whatever happens.' Odd Bod always thought of Timmy first, so did Timmy. Between them, the dog was always well catered for. Timmy stood up and stepped out of his basket.

'You can't quarrel with the inevitable,' he thought. Odd Bod picked up the dog's bed and carried it upstairs. He came down, lifted up his rocking chair and carried that to his bedroom as well. He looked out of the window. It was still pouring with rain. He could see the water butt from where he was. The water was almost to the top. Soon it would overflow.

'I could have seen that coming a mile off,' thought Timmy. 'It takes a dog to recognise these things. That's why we're so intelligent, you see. No doubt about it. It's no good my going on, though. He never takes any notice of me.'

Odd Bod hurried downstairs. He packed all his food, and Timmy's, into a large basket and took that upstairs as well. In no time at all, the kitchen was empty, except for the table, which was too heavy for Odd Bod to carry up by himself. He went upstairs again. Timmy followed him, still wagging his tail. 'Did upstairs have a cooker by any chance? Of course not.'

The bedroom was very crowded. Furniture was piled up, one piece on top of another. Timmy climbed into his basket. Odd Bod sat down in his rocking chair. He rocked himself to and fro and thought about what to do next. Timmy decided to stay where he was. He'd had enough dizzy spells for one day.

There was nothing much Odd Bod could do, in fact. He couldn't stop it raining, that was for sure, but he wasn't really able to think about anything else except the water coming into his house. Presently he stood up and went to the window. He looked out. It seemed as if the worst was about to happen. He watched the water as it poured over the top of the rain butt and crept towards the house. He watched it getting closer and closer and knew that it was no use shutting the kitchen door. The water would only come in underneath.

Just then something remarkable happened. It suddenly stopped raining and the sun came out. Odd Bod looked up. He had been watching the water so intently, he hadn't noticed a break in the clouds. Odd Bod smiled at the sky. He was happy once more, because the sun was shining, the birds had started singing and the water wouldn't come in and spoil his house after all. 'I think I'll make a cup of tea to celebrate,' Odd Bod said to Timmy. 'And you can have a special dish of milk.'

'Better than nothing, I suppose,' thought Timmy, who could easily have won the Most Ungrateful Dog of the

Year Competition. Odd Bod went downstairs for the fourteenth time that morning and started moving all the things back. Timmy followed him. 'I don't know why I didn't realise the butt might have overflowed before,' said Odd Bod.

'Let's face it, some of us are quicker than others,' mused Timmy. 'Sad, but fact.'

'Still, I didn't know it was going to rain so much,' Odd Bod went on.

'Excuses,' thought Timmy. 'Where does he find them all?'

'Anyway, there's one thing I must do before it rains again,' Odd Bod carried on, coming to the point at last. 'Get a bigger rain butt.'

'Soup,' signalled Timmy. 'S-o-u-p. I don't mind what sort it is. Any kind will do, as long as it's thick and hot and nourishing.'

'Otherwise, we'll be in the soup,' said Odd Bod.

Timmy stomped out, lost for words.

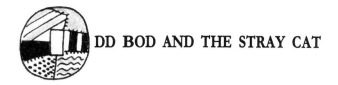# ODD BOD AND THE STRAY CAT

Odd Bod came downstairs one morning. He put the kettle on, as usual, to make his cup of tea. When he looked for the milk, however, there was none to be seen.

He peered out of the window to see whether the milkman had called. In fact he had, but Odd Bod hadn't seen the bottle because, for some reason, the milkman had left it in a different place. Odd Bod opened the back door and, to his surprise, in ran a very beautiful cat. She was so pretty – brown, ginger, black and white. She mewed and rubbed against Odd Bod's legs.

'You are a pretty thing,' said Odd Bod. 'I wonder where you've come from. What's more, I wonder what Timmy will say when he sees you.' Timmy, of course, was not up yet. He knew he was lazy and accepted the fact. If that's the way he was, that's the way he would have to go on being.

Odd Bod went over to the dog's basket. 'Timmy, we have a visitor,' he said, breaking the news as gently as possible. Timmy opened one eye and stretched. What was that the man had said – visitor? Wasn't it rather early in the morning for visitors? Some people had absolutely no consideration. Or was it imagination? The kettle boiled. Odd Bod let it whistle. He was more concerned about the cat and what Timmy would think of her. Timmy finally made it out of his basket. Just. Odd Bod turned the kettle down.

'Now what's all this?' Timmy blinked.

'I'll make the tea, Timmy,' Odd Bod said, 'then we can talk about it.'

'Talk about what?' Timmy wondered. 'He does keep on so.'

Timmy suddenly came to. He realised what Odd Bod had been saying. They had a visitor. What sort of a visitor? Then he saw the cat. 'Oh, *that* sort of visitor,' he thought. Timmy was not overfond of cats. He found them rather silly creatures. Almost as silly as flowers, in fact, which was saying something. He was too lazy to chase them or do anything like that. In any case, he considered it beneath his dignity. Cats were totally exhausting, never still for two seconds. It wore him out just looking at them. They were always jumping out at you, tearing after mice, showing off to an alarming degree. Timmy liked to be quiet and contemplative. 'I expect I was a monk in another life,' he mused. 'Or maybe it was a monk fish. That sounds more like it, if my luck is anything to go by.'

Anyway, for whatever reason, the cats he had met so far, he hadn't thought too much of. When it came to it, quite what could you expect? Cats, in his experience, were out for all they could get. He wasn't, of course. Absolutely not. He liked to be considerate, show affection, when it was earned, that is. Cats were different. They were very strange beings. Aloof. Removed from reality. They always seemed to be out to prove something. Quite what, Timmy wasn't sure, but they could never be relied upon to be the same from one moment to the next. In any case, whoever heard of a telepathic cat? Telepathetic, more likely.

'Timmy, come on now. You're the host,' said Odd Bod. 'Show some manners.'

'Manners indeed!' thought Timmy. 'So early in the

morning. It isn't right. Another thing, I hope there will be enough milk. Cats drink an awful lot.' Timmy was never slow at getting down to basics.

'Timmy, come on,' repeated Odd Bod.

The dog remained where he was. He wasn't quite sure what his next move should be. The decision was taken out of his hands, however, as the cat stood up and came over to Timmy. He wasn't at all certain what was going to happen, but the cat had definitely made the first move. She came right up to Timmy. He sat down in his basket and before he knew what was happening, she had started to lick his ear. Timmy blinked. He wasn't used to this kind of thing at all. 'Different,' he thought to himself, when he had recovered from his surprise. 'And,' he had to admit, 'I must say it wasn't altogether unpleasant. In fact I rather enjoyed it. What next, I wonder?' Once again, the cat was the first to move. She put a paw on Timmy's basket and stepped in beside him.

'Hm,' he thought, 'we *are* friendly.' He had certainly not met a cat like this one before. 'What's she trying to prove this time? If she thinks she's a dog, she can get that thought right out of her head, because she isn't. Absolutely no chance.'

Odd Bod beamed. 'I'm pleased to see you're getting on so well,' he said to them both. 'Now I suppose you'd like some milk.'

'I'd like some,' thought Timmy. 'Point is, will there be any?' Odd Bod poured some milk into Timmy's bowl and put some in a saucer for the cat. 'So far, so good,' thought Timmy. 'At least he had the decency to serve me first. That's one priority he's got right, but how long will it last?' He looked at the cat, then at Odd Bod. Things had been really rather comfortable up until now. Timmy could see big changes ahead. Changes that were definitely not for the better.

'Does she like buttered turnips?' wondered Timmy, all of a sudden. 'No, I shouldn't think so. They're quite an unusual choice, pretty sophisticated. Something a dog would appreciate. Not even all dogs, I might add. Just those with finely tuned taste buds. She's only a cat, after all. Quite entertaining, but still just a cat. Which is

a disability a dog like me simply cannot comprehend.'

'You've certainly made yourself at home,' Odd Bod said to the cat as she started lapping her milk.

'Hasn't she just!' thought Timmy.

He strolled over to his bowl, master of the situation once more, and started to drink. 'Better not take any chances,' he told himself. 'You never know with these cats. As soon as you turn your back, they're as likely to have yours as well as their own. Now that's something a dog would simply never do. It's a good job I've been around a bit, otherwise I could be taken for a nice little ride here. However, this time I'll give her the benefit of the doubt. I know I'm superior. Let's leave it at that. There's no need for me to make a fuss proving it.'

Timmy wondered how long their visitor would be stopping and what the sleeping arrangements were likely to be. He was a dog given to long and elaborate calculations. Would there be enough meat to go round? What were the chances of a second helping? Would there be time to snatch another nap before supper? Would he have to go for yet another walk that evening – if so, how could he possibly get out of it?

'I'm doing myself far more good, curled up in my basket,' he told himself at least six times a day, 'but what about this cat – what are we going to do about her? She seems a nice sort of thing, as cats go,' he went on, trying to persuade himself that he wasn't in the least bit bothered about the whole affair. 'I don't think she'll give me too much trouble. I shan't let her, you see. We'll just have to play it by ear,' and Timmy remembered how nice it had been when she had suddenly licked him.

Odd Bod left the door open, but as the day went by, the cat showed no sign of wanting to leave. 'You can stay as long as you like,' said Odd Bod. 'Can't she, Tim?' Timmy raised an eyebrow. Things could be getting out of hand.

'Fat lot of use asking me,' he thought. 'As if I had any say in the matter. If she wants to stay, you'll let her, no matter what I think. I've seen it all before.' That night, Timmy went to bed in his basket, as usual. The cat climbed in and curled up beside him. Once again she started licking his ear. 'It must be a sign of affection,' thought Timmy. 'I'll have to be careful. A chap could get to like it.'

The next day the cat was still there. Odd Bod fed her, with Timmy. She seemed to have settled in completely. Much to Timmy's relief, there still appeared to be enough food to go round. To his surprise, he found that he had accepted the cat very quickly. This was unusual, because Timmy was not the most adaptable of animals. For example, when he got up in the morning, he went once round the centre flower bed and back into his basket. He was never one to overdo things and always went the same way round. If anything happened to disturb this ritual, it put Timmy out completely and upset him for the rest of the day.

Odd Bod wondered where the cat had come from. He had certainly never seen her before. He didn't like the idea of her not having a home, and as she seemed to like Timmy so much, he hoped that she would stay.

'We must give you a name. Let's see now . . . I think Alice would be suitable.'

'Suitable for what?' wondered Timmy.

'We'll call you Alice,' said Odd Bod. Her stay, however, was to be short lived. When Odd Bod came down the next morning, there was no sign of Alice. 'She's gone, boy,' said Odd Bod. 'Cats are like that.' Timmy looked quite upset.

'That's what comes of being so independent. Obviously didn't know when she was well off. She must have done a midnight flit,' he thought. 'I didn't hear her, though. Probably went through the window. Pity. I'd grown rather fond of her. I mean for a cat. Perhaps she didn't like her name,' Timmy wondered, making straight for his milk. 'Ah well, I've more important things to think about. I mean, fancy worrying about a cat. That's carrying things just a bit too far.'

DD BOD GOES TO THE TRAVEL AGENT

Odd Bod had forgotten all about the holiday. He had had so much on his mind. The Flower Festival. The decorating. Alice's fleeting visit. And all that trouble with the rain butt. Then suddenly Odd Bod remembered. 'You're looking a bit peeky, Tim.'

'There's something very wrong with me if I am. Since when did I have a flat face and permanent snuffles? Now if you'd said Labrador or Red Setter, that would be different, but I can't see how you can liken me to a Pekinese, really I can't.'

'I suppose we had better do something about this holiday,' said Odd Bod. 'Coming boy?'

'Might as well,' thought Timmy. 'Show willing, as it were. If he has any decisions to make, he could probably do with a second mind, especially with the way his seems to work.' Timmy instantly forgot about the insult and stepped out of his basket with a sprightliness rarely to be seen. 'I wonder where we'll end up,' mused the dog as he trotted along, not even bothering to attend to the enticing smells en route. They arrived at the travel shop and went in.

'Good morning,' said the girl, who was rearranging the brochures. 'Can I help you?'

'I want, that is we want, to go somewhere sunny,' said Odd Bod. 'Are there such places?'

'We have flights to Italy, Spain, Greece and Yugoslavia,' said the girl. 'They're all nice and sunny.'

'We wouldn't want to fly anywhere. Timmy wouldn't like that.'

Timmy looked up. 'Chance would be a fine thing,' he thought.

'You wouldn't want to fly, Tim. All crated up. And then I wouldn't get you back for six months.'

'Sounds like a good deal,' thought Timmy. 'A really long holiday.'

'No, I meant in this country,' continued Odd Bod to the girl.

'That's different,' she said. 'Altogether different. You've got the pick. You're just as likely to get sun in one part as another.'

'That's true,' said Odd Bod.

'If I were you, though, I'd go to Mickleham-on-Sea. It's a small resort, so you get a higher share of whatever sun is going.'

'If he swallows that, he'll believe anything,' Timmy observed.

'That makes sense. Yes, I can see that.'

'He's worse than I thought.' Timmy looked up at Odd Bod again.

'It's not too commercialised,' continued the girl. 'Quite unspoilt. There aren't too many of them left.'

'And there can't be too many loons who would believe a story like that,' thought Timmy.

'We have a guest house there that's particularly friendly. It's run by Mrs Backbent, a widow lady. She won't mind taking your friend.'

Timmy bristled. '*She* won't mind, indeed! Maybe I shall mind going there. I'm very particular where I put my paws.'

'Timmy's no trouble, are you boy?'

Timmy looked. 'Fawning again,' he thought. 'You won't get round me as easily as that.'

'We include the train fare, so it makes it cheaper. Will it be for one week or two?'

'Just the one,' said Odd Bod. 'See how we go. We may not like it.'

'Oh you will,' said the girl.

'Indeed,' thought Timmy. 'A little presumptuous, aren't we?'

'Are there good beaches?' asked Odd Bod. 'Timmy

likes a good run before breakfast.'

'Do I? First I've heard of it.'

'Don't you, boy?'

'Don't I what?' Timmy had forgotten the original question, or maybe he was being unusually obtuse. He gave his paw a quick lick, for something to do as much as anything. He was getting rather bored with the proceedings and hoped that the holiday, if and when it came, would be worth it all.

'Yes, right. Mickleham it is,' said Odd Bod.

'Nice to be consulted. I suppose I will have to go along with it, as usual, since I clearly have no say in the matter,' Timmy went on to himself.

When they arrived home, Odd Bod started on the packing. There were several days to go before it was time to catch the train, but Odd Bod liked to be prepared well in advance. He fetched the large carpet bag down from the loft, together with Timmy's collapsible bed, and started collecting things together.

Everything was everywhere, spread out on the kitchen floor, as it usually was when Odd Bod did something like this, in an attempt to make up his mind what to take with him on holiday. It was so long since he last did any packing that he was scared of leaving something vital behind and not having enough when he got there. The kitchen looked like a second hand clothes shop.

Timmy watched from a safe distance and decided not to offer help in any way. 'If I'd known there would be all this fuss, I wouldn't have suggested the idea,' thought Timmy. 'I'd be just as happy at home,

speaking for myself that is. As far as I'm concerned, the garden is one long holiday for me.'

'It'll be all right when we get there, boy,' said Odd Bod.

'Can we be sure of that? And will there be buttered turnips, might one enquire? I doubt it. It'll be all fish, I expect. Bound to be, by the sea. And I don't intend changing into a cat, even for a week. Anyway, if we go on like this, it will be time to come home before we've even started out. And I'll be back to chasing my own tail again.'

Finally, the last just-in-case item was stowed carefully in the bag. 'Now have we forgotten anything?' Odd Bod asked.

'You may have, but as far as I can remember, I haven't,' thought Timmy. 'The kitchen sink is fixed, otherwise that might go. So yes, I imagine that this should be about it. For a week, that is. Any longer and I suppose we might have to think again.'

'Perhaps my galoshes,' said Odd Bod. 'You never know. Sun can be very contrary.'

'The sun isn't the only one,' thought Timmy.

'It's going to be good, boy. All that sea air. You'll be really fit,' said Odd Bod. Timmy climbed into his basket. He could feel a little sleep coming on and didn't want to have to move, once it arrived. Just to make his point quite clear, he yawned. 'Tired boy?'

'No, just giving my mouth an airing. Making sure my jaws still work. Getting ready for all that sea air,' thought the dog.

'Perhaps you'd like something to eat?' Timmy was

instantly on the alert. 'We're getting a little low, Tim. I don't want to leave too much food around while we're away.'

'I hadn't noticed there was all that much to leave,' thought Timmy. 'Not even while we're here, let alone when we're not. There never seems to be enough to me. However, I imagine I might be able to toy with something. If I force myself.'

'Here you are, as a special treat, you can have some of my stew,' said Odd Bod.

'Very aptly named, I should say. Still, I daresay I could manage it.'

'It's nice and hot.'

Unlike most dogs, Timmy preferred his food to be on the warm side. Odd Bod ladled a very generous portion into Timmy's bowl and gave some to himself. Timmy finished first, as usual. His food went straight down to his stomach, without touching the sides. 'How about a little walk?' asked Odd Bod. 'Get us into training for the seaside.' Timmy looked at his basket, longingly. 'It's a beautiful evening, boy. We'd better get the last of the day.'

'As long as it doesn't last too long. I'm not all that fond of this walking into the sunset lark.'

'Coming, boy?' Odd Bod persisted.

'Oh am I? Yes, I suppose I must be. It rather looks like it, doesn't it? That's two walks in one day. I hope he's not going to make a habit of this. I'll start fading away or something. I'm sure it's not good for me.' Timmy glared at the sun, willing it to sink quickly.

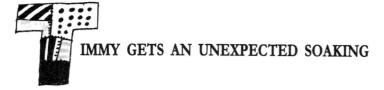

TIMMY GETS AN UNEXPECTED SOAKING

The day before they were due to depart on their holiday, Odd Bod gave Timmy the news that he knew would not be particularly welcome. 'You must have a bath before we go, boy.'

'There's always a drawback,' thought Timmy. 'I've noticed it time and time again.'

Just about more than anything else, Timmy hated having a bath. If he were honest, it was one thing he envied cats for – the fact that they rarely seemed to be given a bath. 'What's their secret, I'd like to know, not that they'd ever tell me. Far too superior, cats.'

'It won't take long, Tim, and we can't have any complaints.'

'Complaints – who said anything about complaints – what's that supposed to mean? When have I ever complained? Tell me that. It's not in my nature.' Odd Bod fetched the tin bath from the shed and half filled it with a mixture of hot and cold water.

'Ready then? Let's take off your collar.' Timmy didn't move. Odd Bod went over to him. 'Come on. The sooner you're in, the sooner you'll be out. You never know, I might find something for you.'

'Might. *Might*. There's a catch here somewhere. Do I fall for it though? Oh let's get it over with.' Timmy dragged himself over to the bath. Odd Bod had laid out Timmy's special shampoo, brush and towel, and put an old waterproof sheet around himself.

'That's it. In you go, boy.' Timmy stepped into the bath. He looked around reproachfully at Odd Bod, who was too busy shampooing him to notice. As in all things he did, Odd Bod was very gentle with the dog. In no time at all, Timmy was out of the bath. 'There, that wasn't too bad, was it? Now you're all ready for the holiday. That's a thought – you could have gone in the sea, Tim. We needn't have bothered with the bath, after all.'

'Now he tells me. Typical. If only he would think first, we'd all be better off. Better still, leave all the thinking to me.' Timmy shook himself vigorously. Water went all over the place. The floor was soaking wet.

'If I'd known that was going to happen, I needn't

have bothered to wash it so thoroughly yesterday,' said Odd Bod. He towelled the dog down.

'It's all a question of forward planning.' Timmy's mind was off again and he immediately forgot about any inconvenience the bath might have caused him. 'This living for the moment business is all very well, but it does pay to look ahead. Talking of which . . . is there . . . any er . . . possibility? I think my tummy's rumbling. That bath must have made me hungry. Some buttered turnips could make up for it. Out of the question, no doubt.'

'Oh dear, I'm out of turnips,' said Odd Bod.

'What did I tell you?' thought Timmy.

'I've just remembered, there may be some more in the woodshed.'

'This knife edge existence is no good to man or beast. My nerves must be in shreds,' Timmy complained to himself.

Odd Bod went out into the shed. He fished around and found a sack. Sure enough, there were just two turnips left. Odd Bod brought them in. 'You're in luck,' he said to the dog.

'That's all right this time,' thought Timmy, 'but there's no relying on it, is there? Some people seem to have more than their fair share. Luck can be very capricious.'

Odd Bod started cleaning the oven.

'Like now, for instance. What's he up to?' wondered the dog. 'Anything to put off getting my dinner!'

'Might as well get this done now,' said Odd Bod to himself. 'While I think of it. Then it will be all clean for when we go away.' The turnips sat on the draining board, waiting their turn.

'Sounds like one of his more ridiculous ideas. If we're not here, there'll be no one to see it, so what's the point in cleaning it? I take it nobody is coming in to cook, while we are away.'

Odd Bod scrubbed and polished. Soon the cooker was sparkling. It looked just like new.

'That's more like it,' said Odd Bod.

'More like what?' wondered Timmy. 'More like a cooker? How can it be more like it when that's what it was in the first place?'

Odd Bod suddenly saw the turnips. 'Dear me, what are those doing there? I must have brought them in by mistake. They make the place so untidy, especially when I've cleaned it all.' Odd Bod put the turnips away in a cupboard.

'I don't believe it.' Timmy was beside himself. 'I am simply not believing this.' He flopped into his basket, exhausted with all the nervous tension. 'If only I could look after myself, things would be very different. You wouldn't catch me cleaning cookers before going on holiday, I can tell you. No good trying a signal, I suppose. Shouldn't think so. He can't keep the thoughts he's got, let alone receive new ones.'

'You must be hungry, boy.'

'No more than usual,' thought Timmy.

'I'd forgotten you hadn't eaten. What would you like? I've seen some turnips around somewhere, but I can't remember where I put them.'

'If you don't know, I'm not telling you,' thought Timmy. 'Bothered if I am.'

As Odd Bod opened the cupboard door to put away his cleaning things, the turnips fell out. 'Look what I've found,' he said. 'That's all right, then. I quite thought you'd have to have parsnips.'

Timmy paused. He was surprised that Odd Bod managed to remember anything.

'Won't be long, boy.'

'Give or take six weeks,' thought the dog and disappeared into the garden, disgusted with the whole affair.

In due course, Odd Bod filled Timmy's dish and put his supper down for him. Timmy reappeared, on cue. 'You're just in time. Well done, boy,' Odd Bod greeted him.

Timmy looked at his bowl. 'So they are,' he thought. 'I know I like my bacon crispy, but this is overdoing things a bit.'

'There you are,' smiled Odd Bod. 'Bacon with buttered turnips. Make the most of them. You may not get any more for a while.'

'No need to make such a song and dance about it. They've been such a long time coming, I quite thought we'd *been* on holiday.' Timmy refused to show any enthusiasm for the meal. He was in one of his moods all of a sudden, and there was no shifting him. He licked half heartedly at the side of the dish. 'Passable, I suppose, considering the time they've been cooking. Then, what can you expect?' Odd Bod always did his best, but there was no pleasing Timmy.

'You're lucky to get them, Tim,' said Odd Bod.

'Don't I know it,' thought the dog. 'There's no need to rub it in.' Finally, his mood evaporated. Chomping began in earnest and the turnips disappeared as quickly as Christmas Day.

'I'm sorry there isn't any more,' said Odd Bod.

'You're sorry,' thought Timmy. 'How do you think *I* feel?'

'Perhaps you'd like a bone.'

'Try me.' Timmy looked. Watched for Odd Bod to make the first move. Waited. Somehow, he couldn't stop his paw from going up to Odd Bod's knee. He hated begging. He knew that most dogs did it, but he liked to be above such things. Most of the time he was, but he did have the occasional lapse. This was just such a one. Odd Bod found the bone in the oven. 'How did it get there?' he asked.

'Don't look at me,' thought Timmy. 'I can't open doors. At least, not that one. Shows how thoroughly the oven must have been cleaned, though.'

Odd Bod went out to the shed to get the yard broom. 'I'll just give the path a quick sweep,' he said. Timmy settled down to review the day.

'Has anything actually been achieved?' he wondered. 'If so, what, and am I any different at the end of it? A little wiser, perhaps. If that's possible.'

Before he could find the answers to any more of his questions, he was almost asleep. 'That's what comes of having a clear conscience,' he thought, just as he finally dropped off.

DD BOD AND TIMMY GO PLACES

Odd Bod and Timmy arrived in plenty of time for their holiday train. They were in fact about forty minutes early. Odd Bod had ordered a car for 9.15 in the morning. 'We might as well do things in style, boy.'

'No reason why not,' thought Timmy, 'except that we rarely do. Better make the most of it while it lasts, I suppose.'

Odd Bod found their place on the train. Timmy was supposed, for some reason, to go in the guard's van. 'I'm not having that,' Odd Bod said. 'You're coming in with me.' Timmy sat down at Odd Bod's feet, and soon they were off. Timmy couldn't see very well from where he was. He tried a paw, but Odd Bod wasn't having him on the seat.

'It's not allowed, Timbo,' he said, as diplomatically as he could. However, he relented later on. 'There's nobody else in the compartment. Your paws are dry and you did have a bath yesterday, so you might as well. Up you get, then.' The journey was uneventful, and after going over the last level crossing, they approached Mickleham. 'I can see the sea,' said Odd Bod. 'Look, Tim!'

'There's no need to get so excited about it. It's only water,' thought Timmy.

Three cars were lined up outside the station. Odd Bod opened the door of the one nearest him. 'Don't let him on the seat,' said the driver. 'I don't like dogs.'

'Wouldn't dream of it, would we, Tim?' whispered Odd Bod. Timmy withered both the man and Odd Bod with one of his special looks, calculated to kill.

'I know what we would do, given half a chance. In any

case, I'm not too fond of drivers with cars like this one.'
They settled in and the car drove off.

'I shan't give him a tip.' Odd Bod whispered in
Timmy's ear.

'Would you have done anyway?' wondered Timmy.
'It's not like you to give money away unnecessarily.'
The car pulled up outside a neat bungalow with

shiny green gates, a very trim lawn and an army of gnomes scattered around. 'Sunnyside' the sign proclaimed. There was a gnome pushing a wheelbarrow, one with his hands in his pockets, doing nothing. Another was sitting on a mushroom, apparently fishing, without much hope, in the green river. A heron was perched nearby. An owl sat awkwardly in a stone shoe.

'Dear me,' said Odd Bod. 'I feel quite claustrophobic. All these funny people.'

'I think I'm going to be sick,' contributed Timmy. 'I do hope not – I shall be in trouble if I am.'

Odd Bod rang the bell. It chimed daintily within. A lady answered the door. 'Mrs Backbent?' Odd Bod enquired, brightly.

'I'm not likely to be anybody else now, am I? Not living here, I mean.'

'I suppose not,' agreed Odd Bod, somewhat deflated.

'Well, come in, won't you. Is this your dog?'

'I would hardly have picked up a stray to bring on holiday, would I?'

'Quite so,' said Mrs Backbent. She spoke with a Northern accent and had one eye that looked at you and one that didn't quite. 'I'll show you your room. The animal will sleep outside, I suppose?'

'He's not used to that,' said Odd Bod. 'I'd rather have him in with me.'

'It's most irregular. I won't have him on the bed.'

Timmy looked. 'Might one enquire who has been sleeping in the bed? Best not to ask, I imagine. You wouldn't catch me on it, that's all I can say.'

'You don't have to worry about Timmy, he's very good mannered, aren't you, boy?' Timmy gave one of his best sniffs.

'In any case, I have brought his basket along, so he'll be quite comfortable.'

'Dinner's at 7.30.'

'Is it possible to have it at half past six?'

'Out of the question,' said Mrs Backbent. 'I have my schedule to keep. And there are my other guests to consider.'

'How many do you have staying at the moment?' Odd Bod asked.

'Just you two, but there might have been others. One can't take chances.'

'Yes, I see,' said Odd Bod.

'I'll show you your room.'

'Oh that's nice,' said Odd Bod. 'Look, Tim, roses on the curtains. And on the walls. And on the bed cover.' Timmy yawned. 'You're like me, you must like roses, Mrs Backbent.'

'Not particularly. They were a special offer. Discontinued. In any case, I hardly ever come in here. I suppose he'll have to have something to eat?'

'He's very fond of buttered turnips,' said Odd Bod.

Mrs Backbent frowned. 'Is he, though? Will he want them for dinner? I call it high tea, actually, on account of the table being rather tall and my having to wear high heels when I'm serving it.'

'If it's possible.'

'I suggest you make it a priority,' thought Timmy.

'I've brought his dish. Here it is.' Odd Bod rummaged in his carpet bag and pulled out a red china bowl.

'That's rather too good for a dog, I would have thought,' Mrs Backbent commented.

'Nothing but the best for Timmy. He likes good ones.'

'I hope these turnips aren't a lot of bother,' said Mrs Backbent. My pans aren't used to cooking for dogs.'

'He likes a bit of meat with them,' said Odd Bod.

'Does he now?' replied Mrs Backbent. 'Does he now?'

After the meal, Odd Bod thought they might have a stroll by the sea. Timmy thought his basket looked very inviting. Odd Bod won.

'Just a quick one,' he said. 'Breath of sea air. Do you the world.'

'Do me in, I wouldn't wonder.'

'She doesn't seem very friendly, boy. Perhaps she's missing her husband.'

'Or a marble or two,' thought the dog. 'That could explain it, I suppose.'

'I don't like it very much here,' said Odd Bod as they walked along. 'We'd be better off at home.'

'What did I tell you? What *did* I tell you? He always wants to be where he isn't.'

'I think we'll go home tomorrow, what do you think, Tim?'

Timmy wasn't thinking anything, for a change. He gauged it was best to let things take their course. It was beginning to get dark. Odd Bod decided that it was time to turn round. 'Nice beach, boy. Pity about Mrs Backbent.'

'You can't have everything,' thought Timmy, philosophically. 'Well, maybe you have to leave home to realize you had most of it all the time. Her buttered turnips left a lot to be desired, I do know that.'

'We didn't see much sea, that's for sure,' said Odd Bod, opening the gate of Sunnyside. He rang the bell. Mrs Backbent answered it.

'I usually lock the door at 9 o'clock,' she said. 'It's five past. You'll have to do better than that tomorrow. Will you be requiring a cooked breakfast?'

'Yes please,' said Odd Bod.

'What about *him*?'

'Timmy likes his bacon nice and crispy and his egg sunny side up. We'd like a car at 8.30, please, if you would be so kind.'

'Does that mean you will be out for luncheon?'

'It does rather. And dinner. Or high or low tea. For the rest of the week.'

'Very well. I'll wish you goodnight.'

The bed Odd Bod had proved to be extremely uncomfortable. Timmy was luckier with his, and snored all night long. The next morning they had breakfast.

'Thank you for a very . . . er . . . pleasant stay, Mrs . . . that is . . . Backbent,' said Odd Bod, doing his best to summon a social grace or two.

'You off then? But you've only just arrived.'

'Yes. How time flies, as they say.'

'Do they now? I've never found it myself. Have you signed the Visitors' Book?'

'I haven't. No, not yet. I couldn't conjure up anything to say. And I didn't think we stayed long enough to make much of a read.' The car came. Odd Bod and Timmy took their leave of Sunnyside. Mrs Backbent did not wave them off. 'The only sunny thing about it is the name,' said Odd Bod. 'It's a pity holidays seem so short.'

'Some shorter than most,' thought Timmy.

'The good thing is they don't take so long to get over,' continued Odd Bod. 'Pity I paid for the week in advance, but it was worth it to escape from Mrs B. Next time we'll go under our own steam. At least I cleaned the cooker, though.'

'If we'd flown,' thought Timmy, 'goodness knows where we'd be by now.'

'I think we should have flown,' said Odd Bod. 'Italy perhaps. Or Greece, maybe.'

'Do you know, I think you're right,' agreed Timmy. 'For once.'

'Not with that travel agent, though.'

'Possibly not,' thought Timmy, who had curled up in his proper basket and was having a bad dream about crates of turnips that were being flown to Yugoslavia by mistake, and eggs that didn't look particularly sunny.

'We'll know another time.'

'Will we?' wondered Timmy. 'I doubt it. Can I let you know? I'm a little busy at the moment.'

ODD BOD AND THE HOMEMADE BREAD

In the village where Odd Bod lived, there was one shop that baked really good bread. It was delicious. If you were up early enough in the morning, you could smell the bread cooking.

One day, Odd Bod went to collect his usual loaf. He liked it fresh and crusty, and went every other day to buy a new one. On this particular day, however, Odd Bod was later than customary and the shop had sold out. 'There's a thing,' said Odd Bod. 'Now what will I do? I've no bread at all in the house.'

'I've some yeast,' said the lady behind the counter. 'You could always bake your own.'

'That's an idea,' replied Odd Bod. 'Is it easy?'

'Oh yes,' said the lady. 'I've made my own bread for years.'

'Hm,' said Odd Bod, doubtfully. 'I could have a go, I suppose. All right, I'll take some yeast please. I'd better have some buns as well, in case the bread doesn't work.'

'You don't know what you can do until you try.'

'Very true,' agreed Odd Bod. 'Or what you can't, of course,' he added, thinking of one or two occasions when he had bitten off rather more than he could chew. He paid the lady for the yeast and buns and went next door to buy flour. 'How to make good bread,' he read on the pack. 'That's all I need, and maybe a little luck.' Once home, he told Timmy what he was going to do.

Timmy gave one of his sniffs. It wasn't meant unkindly. Whatever Timmy thought to himself about Odd Bod, it was never meant maliciously. Timmy was devoted to him really. On his own terms. In his own way. He was a cautious sort of dog and didn't like it when he felt Odd Bod behaved foolishly. He knew that Odd Bod had never made bread before and was doubtful whether he would be able to manage it successfully. 'Clear as you go, my mother always used to say,' said Odd Bod to Timmy, before he had even started. 'Clear as you go.'

'I agree,' thought Timmy, 'but it never seems to be very popular when I do it. Look at the time I dug up all those flowers that were in the way. There was a terrible fuss. I don't know why. They'd been there long enough, if you ask me. And that meat I came across, quite by accident, you understand. I didn't know it had been put out for a special purpose. I know it's unlikely, but it could have been for me.'

Odd Bod started to whistle. It was the one thing that drove Timmy out of the house. Odd Bod didn't ever seem to notice that every time he started whistling, Timmy made for the door. He didn't want to upset Odd Bod by making a fuss, so he used to get up and walk out casually, then run out of earshot as quickly as possible. It wasn't because Odd Bod's whistling was always out of tune. It was, of course, but Timmy could put up with that. It was more the monotony and the fact that it was very high pitched and always the same tune – Cherry Ripe.

As usual, Timmy sloped off into the garden. 'That should just about do it,' thought the dog, coming to the far edge of the lawn. 'Can't hear much from here. I don't know though. Maybe over there. Yes, that's better. Perfect.'

Odd Bod read the instructions. He mixed the yeast with the warm water and sugar. 'That doesn't look like enough yeast,' he said, doubling the quantity, just to make sure. He left it all to start bubbling. When the mixture was nice and frothy, he added in the flour and salt and the rest of the water, squeezing it all together.

'There's nothing to this,' said Odd Bod, whistling to himself. 'I don't think I'll ever go back to buying shop bread, however good it may be.' Timmy reappeared, thinking that the whistling might have stopped, only to find that it had started up again. He retreated once more into the peace of the garden.

The birds were singing. 'That's more like it,' thought Timmy, stretching out in the sun. 'Anything's preferable to that noise.'

Odd Bod kneaded the dough very thoroughly. He

threw it about, knocking it this way and that. 'I'm really rather enjoying this,' he said to himself. 'You don't know what you're missing, boy,' he called to Timmy. Timmy rather thought he did. He grunted a half-hearted reply.

'I wouldn't mind some milk,' he thought. 'Even better, some buttered turnips. Followed perhaps by some cider baked gammon, nothing too elaborate, but I am rather partial to that. Yes, that would be quite acceptable, thank you very much. But please don't go to a lot of trouble on my account. I always say I eat to live. In this establishment, it wouldn't pay to approach things the other way round.'

Timmy was very rude about Odd Bod's cooking, with small cause, as Odd Bod was always out to provide him with something tasty, and Timmy had very little room to complain. The dog, however, saw it differently. 'Oh he tries,' Timmy thought. 'A thousand times a day, but what does it amount to?'

The whistling continued from within. 'Now he's making this bread. Goodness knows how long it will take. No wonder people take the rise out of him. I mean, he asks for it. He'll be putting it in my milk next.'

'You can have some of this in your milk, boy. When it's baked,' Odd Bod called into the garden. 'You'll like that.'

'Will I now?' wondered Timmy. 'That wasn't meant to be a message. Why don't I keep my big mind shut and why does this telepathy thing only work when I don't want it to? I'd better send out another signal to cancel the one that slipped out in error . . .'

'Some milk would be nice. Plain, ordinary milk. Preferably cold . . .'

'Enough to make three loaves,' Odd Bod read on the packet. 'That should be enough to keep us going, boy.'

'For ever,' Timmy thought. His hearing was very acute. He could pick up everything perfectly when he chose.

Odd Bod put the dough back into the bowl and covered it with a cloth. 'Bread's all right,' thought Timmy. 'Like everything else, in moderation, as long as you have something with it. Something, that is, except milk. I mean, I don't go much on it by itself.'

'Leave in a warm place,' Odd Bod read on the packet. 'I'll put it on top of the stove. That's nice and hot. Perhaps it will make the dough rise more quickly.' Odd Bod went out into the garden. He started weeding some plants. Very soon, he had forgotten about the bread. All of a sudden, he looked at his watch. An hour had gone past. Twice as long as the packet had said. He rushed inside.

'There's a thing,' he said, as he looked at the stove. The dough had risen all right. It had risen so much it had run over the top of the bowl. Over the top and

down the sides. It was now oozing very nicely all over the stove. 'Dear me,' said Odd Bod, 'I must have put in too much yeast after all. I'll bake this anyway and see what happens.' Odd Bod put the dough in a tin and the tin into the oven. He set the pinger to remind him when the bread would be done. This time he was leaving nothing to chance.

Once again, Odd Bod went out into the garden. He started watering his flowers. 'Now I could have done that,' thought Timmy, helpfully. 'Saved you a job.' After a while, the pinger pinged. Odd Bod heard it and rushed inside. He took the bread out of the oven. The loaf certainly looked good. Odd Bod wasn't too sure how it would taste. At supper that evening, he cut himself a large slice. It was, in fact, very good.

'At least I have one loaf. But that's one instead of three,' Odd Bod said to Timmy. 'I won't try to be so clever the next time.'

'Hm,' thought Timmy. 'I'll believe that when the next time comes. I wonder if there's any milk. As we seem to be rather short of bread.'

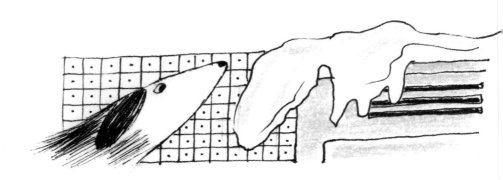

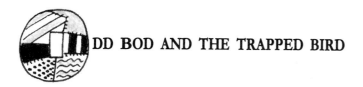# ODD BOD AND THE TRAPPED BIRD

Odd Bod had a thing about birds.

He couldn't bear to have them too near him. They were all right flying about or hopping in his garden, and he always remembered to put out plenty of food for them in the winter. His biggest fear, however, was that one would get into his house.

He couldn't understand why he didn't like them. With some people it was spiders, with others it was moths, but Odd Bod could handle both spiders and moths with no trouble at all. Others were afraid of mice. Not Odd Bod. He was very fond of mice. Anything with fur was all right. But feathers – they were another matter entirely.

One day Odd Bod was in his kitchen, pouring Timmy some milk, when suddenly he looked up. There on the window sill was a small brown bird. It must have been quite young. Odd Bod jumped out of his skin. 'Just what I didn't want to happen,' he thought to himself. 'However did it get there? More to the point, how am I going to get it out again?'

Odd Bod thought for a minute. It was no use sitting in his rocking chair, which is what he usually did when he wanted to work something out. He would never stay calm enough to think, not with the bird in the same room. Odd Bod could feel the back of his neck go tense and his skin was hot.

It couldn't stay there, though, that was for sure. This wouldn't be good for the bird and it certainly wasn't good for him. Odd Bod thought some more. The best thing to do would be to open as many doors and windows as possible and hope that the bird would fly away. He started with the kitchen door, gingerly at first, then gradually pushed it right open. The bird did not move, much to Odd Bod's relief, as he was so close to it. Then he opened the window. 'That should do it,' he thought. 'It's a good job you're not a cat,' Odd Bod said to Timmy.

Timmy just looked at Odd Bod. 'A what? What was the man on about?' He couldn't believe his ears. 'Who in their right mind would ever think of being a cat? Good job indeed.' Timmy was extremely put out at being mentioned in the same breath as such a creature. Erring on the side of generosity for a change, he supposed that Odd Bod must be suffering from some kind of mental eruption and had had an unfortunate relapse.

Odd Bod crept over to the window. The bird cheeped

and hopped closer into the corner, out of harm's way. Odd Bod's glasses, now completely steamed up, slipped down his nose and clung rather precariously to the end of it. 'So far, so good,' said Odd Bod, doing his best to make a dignified recovery.

'So far, very boring,' thought Timmy, his generous interlude soon over. 'I don't know which is worse, birds or flowers. Flowers, I think. At least birds go off eventually. Flowers stay rooted to the spot. You can't budge them. I should know, I've tried often enough.'

Very carefully, Odd Bod reached closer to the bird to open the other window. He closed his eyes while doing it in order not to see the bird. In doing so, he missed the catch and put his hand straight through a pane of glass. Blood spurted from a large cut. Odd Bod put his

other hand in his pocket and pulled out a handkerchief. He bound it round his hand as best he could. 'There's a thing,' he said, opening one eye. The bird flew up at the sound of the breaking glass. Odd Bod knocked his glasses off his nose. 'Oh bother the bird,' he said, bending down, trying to find them again. They had fallen into Timmy's water bowl.

'Shouldn't meddle,' thought the dog.

Odd Bod wiped his glasses dry and put them on again. 'First clean they've had for weeks, I shouldn't wonder,' Timmy observed. 'It's an ill wind, isn't that what they say?' The bird had returned to its original position. It sat there, trembling.

'He's as frightened of me as I am of him,' Odd Bod said.

'Can you blame it?' wondered Timmy. 'All that fussing and fidgeting.'

'I'll go out into the garden and leave him to it,' Odd Bod said to Timmy. 'Coming, boy?' Timmy heaved himself out of his basket. He couldn't understand why Odd Bod was making such a commotion. It was only a bird after all. Then Odd Bod had one of his sudden thoughts. 'I'll put some bread on the bird table. Perhaps the bird will fly out after it,' he said to Timmy.

'A pig might,' thought the dog.

Quite what Odd Bod hoped this might achieve is hard to imagine, as the bird table couldn't be seen from where the bird was. It wasn't Odd Bod's fault that he wasn't very practical, just the way he was made. Some people were practical. Odd Bod definitely was not.

'Hm,' thought Timmy. 'Waste of good bread, I should say. That would have been very tasty fried. If he waits, which I know he won't, the bird will go away of its own accord. He hasn't any patience, of course. What man has? I mean, think of the time I spend waiting for him to get my food ready. Hours sometimes. Days. Weeks even. I feel pretty weak, but do I complain? Of course not.' Odd Bod went inside to fetch the bread. 'It wouldn't do any good if I did,' Timmy went on to himself. 'No, I don't think you'll find there are too many dogs as patient as I. Or as long suffering.'

The bird was in exactly the same position. It hadn't moved an inch or even a centimetre. 'Bother,' said Odd Bod.

'Failed again,' pronounced Timmy, instant judgment, as always, at the ready.

Odd Bod went to the bread bin, took out the loaf and cut off a large slice. It was about ten times bigger than the bird. 'There, that ought to do it,' he said to himself, with unusual optimism. He glared at the bird from a safe distance and took the bread into the garden, waving it above his head as he went, to make it as visible as possible. Odd Bod wasn't in a bad mood exactly. He just wanted the bird out of the house, so that he could get on with what he was doing, whatever that was. He broke up the bread and put it on the bird table. 'Now we'll see what happens,' he said to Timmy, who by this time was trying to get to sleep under the apple tree. The whole affair was so unbelievably boring. In any case, it didn't ever take Timmy long to drop off.

81

He obviously wasn't going to get anything to eat all the time that bird was around, so he might just as well go to sleep. If it wasn't flowers it was cats, if it wasn't cats it was birds. There was always something to take Odd Bod's attention away from Timmy's requirements. The dog was also rather ashamed of Odd Bod for making such a fuss. Going to sleep seemed the only thing to do. 'I don't blame you,' said Odd Bod. 'If it weren't for that wretched bird, I'd probably do the same.'

Timmy put a paw over one ear. He was not in the mood for excuses. Odd Bod went inside yet again. He closed his eyes and thought that he would count up to ten. 'When I open my eyes, the bird will be gone,' said Odd Bod embarking upon what appeared to be the start of a very Timmy-like superstitious sequence. Odd Bod counted up to ten and opened his eyes. He looked across at the window ledge. There was no sign of the bird. 'There, what did I tell you,' said Odd Bod to himself. He walked over to the window. Unfortunately, he had spoken too soon and the spell, charm, call it what you will, had not worked. The bird was still there. It had moved behind the curtain and was standing trembling more than ever.

'This is ridiculous,' said Odd Bod. Then all of a sudden there was a flapping of wings. Before he knew what was happening, the bird had flown from the window ledge and perched right on top of Odd Bod's head. For a second he froze. When he recovered himself from the shock, he found that the bird did not really bother him at all. 'Now if you can just get outside with it, the bird

will be free,' he told himself. Very slowly, Odd Bod began moving towards the open door.

'There,' said Odd Bod to the bird as he stepped out into the garden. 'Now you are free.' Timmy had woken up. The bird was still on Odd Bod's head. 'Don't you think I'm brave, Tim?' Timmy yawned.

'What did I tell you?' thought the dog. 'Wicked waste. That bread would have made a very nice pudding. I'm quite partial to bread pudding. Not that I get it often, of course.'

The bird still seemed disinclined to move. 'It likes me, Timmy,' said Odd Bod.

'The man's a fool,' thought Timmy. The bird cheeped and flew off into the summer air.

'That wasn't so bad. Now I can have my sleep after all,' said Odd Bod to no one in particular.

'It's all right for some,' thought Timmy, 'but what about my breakfast? If you ask me, he gets lazier every day. Ah well, these things are sent to try us, I suppose. They say there's one born every minute. One what, I'd like to know. It's not a dog, that's for sure. There'd be some sense in that, and the world would be a saner place if it were.'

'Rocking chair or rockery?' Odd Bod asked himself.

'What's he on about now?' sighed the dog.

'Rocking chair, I think. In case it rains. It will keep me moving, then I won't get so wet.'

'He's off his rocker all right. Sad, but there it is,' and Timmy dismissed the whole affair.

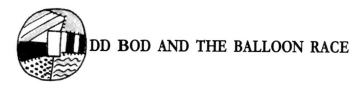# ODD BOD AND THE BALLOON RACE

Odd Bod was out in his garden one day, picking roses. He looked up at the sky. It was getting dark, very dark indeed. All of a sudden, he saw three beautiful balloons sailing over his cottage. He had never seen them so close before. Odd Bod loved balloons. Loved to think what it would feel like to go floating over the rooftops. Loved their bright colours and the way they moved so quietly, silent except for the sound of their burners.

The men in one balloon waved to Odd Bod. Odd Bod waved back. There was always something very special about people in balloons, he thought. They had a kind of magic about them. A magic that came from their being able to go to places that he had never seen.

Timmy ran out into the garden and barked at the balloons. He couldn't understand how they could go by so quietly. Usually things that moved made a lot of noise. He barked at those too, of course. Cars, buses, milkmen, trains . . . Anything that came too near. He barked at the balloons because they were different. This close to the house, they were also rather large. Odd Bod watched them out of sight, rather wistfully. He went inside to make a cup of tea. He put the kettle on and came outside again. It was even darker than before. Just then it thundered. Timmy ran in.

'That's quite enough of that,' he thought. Thunder was one thing he really could not stand, besides flowers, that is, but at least they kept quiet. If there were any noises to be made, Timmy liked to be the one making them. He always felt that thunder took a very unfair advantage. It could always bark louder than he could.

'I guess these will be better inside,' said Odd Bod, putting the roses on the table.

'Do you now?' thought Timmy. 'Can't say I can see much difference myself. They look pretty ridiculous, inside or out. Food always tastes much better outside, it's true, but that's different. I can see some sense in food. That is, I could if I ever got any.'

Odd Bod looked out again to see if there were any more balloons. He felt sorry for the people in them in case a storm was on the way, and went back into the garden. Sure enough, there was one more balloon. It

BARK! BARK!

was even lower than the others. 'If it drops much lower, it will come right down on my cottage,' thought Odd Bod, nervously. He watched it getting closer and closer. The closer it came, the lower it seemed. Odd Bod could see the person very clearly.

'Help, help,' shouted the man. 'Help me, please. I must land. Is this your garden?'

'Yes,' replied Odd Bod, 'but you're quite welcome. You don't want to be up there if a storm's coming.'

'Can you run after the balloon and catch it as I hit the ground?' asked the man.

'I'll try,' said Odd Bod. He ran after the balloon, which knocked him sideways as it reached the ground.

Timmy came rushing out to see what the matter was. 'I knew that it would be too much for him. A man of his age, very undignified.' And he barked even louder than before.

'Quiet, Timmy,' said Odd Bod.

'Oh very well,' thought the dog. 'I was only trying to help. Sometimes I think "quiet" is the only word he knows. Besides "must" that is.'

Odd Bod scrambled up and tried to get hold of the balloon again. This time he was luckier and managed to stay upright. The balloon finally came to rest. Odd Bod held on tightly while the man climbed out. 'Thank you very much for helping me,' he said. 'I'm Guy Roper, by the way. I don't know what I would have done without you. I lost my way in the race, you see.'

Odd Bod smiled.

'Bang go my chances of buttered turnips today,'

thought Timmy. 'Or anything else come to that. His mind will be up in the clouds more than ever. He's bound to forget.'

'I hope I haven't damaged your garden too much,' said the man.

'Oh that's all right,' replied Odd Bod, surprisingly. 'It was more important to get you down. I'm just making a cup of tea. Would you like one?'

'Yes, please,' said Guy. 'That's very kind of you.'

'Not at all,' said Odd Bod. 'This is Timmy, by the way. He does tend to bark rather a lot.'

'Hello, Timmy,' said Guy.

'That's a fine introduction, I must say,' thought the dog. 'I can do other things as well, you know. Especially if I put my mind to it.' Odd Bod and Guy went inside just as the kettle was boiling. Odd Bod made the tea. He put down a large dish of milk for Timmy and took out the spicy cakes he always kept in case someone called. Timmy looked through the milk as if it weren't there.

'Nothing would induce me to touch it,' Timmy went on to himself. 'Anyone would think I liked the stuff, the way he keeps on giving it to me. Anyone would think that I was a cat. And I'm not. Certainly not.'

Guy told Odd Bod the story of how he had set out on the race and how it looked as if a storm would come. Timmy sniffed. 'Rather silly, if you ask me,' he thought. 'Taking off in that thing with no legs. You wouldn't catch me doing it, I can tell you. Still some people will do anything for effect.'

'And then of course I saw your cottage,' said Guy.

Bored with the story so far, Timmy eyed the milk. He sidled up to the dish. 'Well, maybe just a drop. Just one tiny, tiny drop.' The next time Timmy looked at the dish, there wasn't a drop in sight. 'Well I never! How did it get like that?' he asked himself. 'Stupid dish.'

'That didn't take long,' said Odd Bod. 'Anyone would think you liked milk.' Timmy turned his head away. 'Anyway, you're quite safe now,' Odd Bod said to Guy.

'I think the storm has passed,' Guy replied. 'I'd better get started again, otherwise I will never catch up with the others.'

'I'll help you,' offered Odd Bod.

'Thanks very much,' replied Guy. 'And for the tea and cake.'

'What cake?' wondered Timmy. 'I didn't see any cake. There wasn't much of anything else either, as far as I can remember. Still, there never is, in my opinion. Not here at any rate. It seems to me I miss out on quite a bit.'

Odd Bod went out with Guy to the balloon. It was still there, tethered to the ground. It swayed slightly in the breeze. The sky was much lighter. Timmy stood in the doorway, looking. 'He's not going up again, surely!' he thought. 'Is there no end to some people's lunacy?'

'I think you'll be all right now,' said Odd Bod, knowledgeably.

'I wouldn't bank on it,' thought Timmy.

Guy climbed into the balloon. 'Thanks again,' he

said. Odd Bod held on to the basket as Guy prepared to take off. 'I'll unload some of this sand, if you don't mind,' said Guy.

'Yes, that's all right,' replied Odd Bod. 'It'll be good for the garden.'

'It's all right if he does it, of course. It would be a different story if it were me doing something like it. Anyway, throw enough out, and with a bit of luck it will smother a few flowers,' thought Timmy.

'You can let go now,' Guy said.

Odd Bod released the balloon and it started to rise. 'Goodbye,' said Odd Bod. 'I hope you win your race.'

'So do I,' said Guy. 'Goodbye for now.'

Odd Bod waved him out of sight. He would have liked to have gone as well, and taken Timmy with him. Fortunately, he didn't mention anything of the sort to the dog.

Timmy went back into the kitchen and checked his bowl. It was empty. Then he remembered the milk. 'Oh yes, I did have a drop. It was gone in two wags.' He climbed into his basket rather anxiously, half expecting it to take off as soon as he settled inside it. In fact it stayed firmly on the ground and showed no signs of going anywhere. Odd Bod came in. He was very happy. It was the first time for a long while that anybody had dropped in to see him. And the first time ever out of the sky.

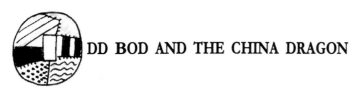ODD BOD AND THE CHINA DRAGON

A fair came to the village where Odd Bod and Timmy lived. It was due to stay for three days. There were roundabouts and dodgems, a big wheel, a caterpillar train, roller coaster, giant helter skelter and all the sideshows you could possibly wish for.

Odd Bod loved fairs. 'We must go,' he said to Timmy. 'Must' was a word Timmy hated more than any other. It never seemed to work in his favour. He thought lunch would be more to the point. Something light perhaps. A little stew maybe. And buttered turnips, of course. They went without saying.

Odd Bod's mind, however, was clearly elsewhere. He could hardly wait until it was evening and time to go. He tried to do his work, but couldn't settle to anything. The day seemed very long. At last he realised his omission. 'I'm sorry, boy. You poor old thing. What can I have been doing? I've forgotten to give you anything to eat.'

Timmy turned his back and sulked in his basket. 'That's great,' he thought. 'It's a bit late to think of food. A bit *too* late in fact. If he thinks I am going to eat now, he has another think coming. I shan't touch a thing.' Timmy could be quite a madam when he put his mind to it and at times was very difficult to live with.

'There you are,' said Odd Bod, putting down the bowl. 'How about that? Will it make up for my forgetfulness?' Timmy stretched a leg, to make out that he had intended getting up anyway, and strolled past the table. He shot an eye at his bowl and glanced over at Odd Bod to see whether he was looking. He was. Timmy waited and cocked an eyebrow. 'Well go on, boy,' said Odd Bod.

'Eat it up. You've waited long enough.'

'You can say that again,' thought the dog.

Timmy struggled. The smell was overpoweringly delicious. 'Perhaps I could, without losing face,' he thought. It was buttered turnips, with pieces of crispy bacon. His number one favourite. 'Just a mouthful, to show willing. They'll only get cold. And then the birds will have them, stupid, twittery things.'

That decided it. Timmy chassied up to his bowl and munched in. 'He's not such a bad stick, after all,' he thought. 'If only he weren't so forgetful. I mean, he does treat me quite well, most of the time, considering he's only a man. A dog would know better of course, but there we are . . . what can you expect?' Timmy finished the final slice, a particularly crispy piece he'd left until last, and even managed a half-hearted wag of his tail in token appreciation. 'There's no need to think you can always win me round with buttered turnips, though, but this time I'm willing to make an exception,' Timmy's mind went on.

At last it was time for the fair to open. Odd Bod and Timmy left the house and walked to the village green where it was being held. 'I've set my heart on winning a china dragon,' said Odd Bod, as they walked along. 'I don't know why. I just have.'

'Now what possible use is a china dragon?' wondered Timmy. 'He does have some funny ideas.' They came to the fair and started walking round. Sure enough, on one of the stalls, among all the other prizes, was a china dragon. It was a very splendid creature. Odd Bod thought it would look really good on his mantelpiece.

'Good evening, please. What do I have to do to win that dragon?' Odd Bod asked the man in charge of the stall.

'Ah, that dragon, sir. It's the only one of its kind in the world. There's not another one like it.'

'Yes, but what do I have to do, please?' asked Odd Bod, impatiently.

'It's quite simple, really. All you have to do is get these three rings over this peg, see.'

The fair man made it sound so easy. Odd Bod took the three rings the man gave him and handed him 30p. He threw the first ring. It landed over the peg. Odd Bod threw the second ring. Once again, it went right over. His pulse started to race. He threw the third ring. This time he wasn't so lucky. It caught on top of the peg, but did not go right over. 'Bother,' said Odd Bod. 'I was too excited.'

'Bad luck, sir,' said the fair man. 'Want to try again?'

'Not today, thank you,' said Odd Bod. 'I'll come back tomorrow.'

Odd Bod went to have a look at the rest of the fair, but his heart was not really in it. In the end, he and Timmy left and went back home.

'Not so much as a sausage,' thought the dog. 'Mind elsewhere, of course, as usual.'

The next day Odd Bod had a lot of things to do. This helped the hours to pass very quickly, which meant that there was not much opportunity to think about the fair. Soon it was time for tea. Odd Bod had other ideas, but remembered just in time to give Timmy his meal. The dog managed to demolish half a large pie, three king size potatoes and some fried marrow, another of his somewhat odd favourites, and was still looking for more. 'Steady now, that's quite enough. You'll get fat,' nagged Odd Bod.

'Fat chance,' thought the dog, 'on what I eat. I mean on what *I* eat, I wonder I haven't faded away completely.'

'Come on, boy,' said Odd Bod. 'You could do with a walk after all that lot.'

'Could I indeed!' thought the dog. 'Do with that lot all over again, more like. Oh well, I suppose I'd better go. I'll never hear the end of it if I don't. Off to that beastly fair again, in search of dragons, no doubt. It's simply not . . . well . . . fair.'

Odd Bod kept hoping he would win the china dragon. It was just what he had always wanted. If only he could get all three rings on the peg, as the man had said. He and Timmy left the house for the second evening running. This time there were more people at the fair. They reached the stall where the dragon had been, but Odd Bod couldn't get anywhere near it. He tried to see whether the dragon was still on show, but it was impossible. Odd Bod was certain somebody had won it, but he couldn't rest until he knew for sure. He decided to come back later when the stall might be less crowded. The two of them wandered about. Odd Bod bought a sausage for himself and one for Timmy. 'Food!' thought the dog. 'Things are looking up.' The sausage was gone in one go.

'Nice while it lasted,' mused the dog. 'But it wasn't long enough to last very long. I'm sure they cut them in half or something. Pity inflation doesn't hit sausages, but then I suppose they would be all air, instead of only half.' Timmy trotted after Odd Bod. Life did seem to be more puzzling the longer you lived it. He flicked his tongue out to make sure no little bits had been missed. No such luck. Soon it would be time for the fair to close. Odd Bod walked back to the stall. From a distance he could see that there were not so many people nearby.

He felt pleased. Now he would be able to see whether the dragon was still to be won. As they drew nearer to the stall, Odd Bod could see why so few people were there. It had closed before the rest. The shutters were up. 'Come on, boy, we may as well go home,' Odd Bod said to Timmy, sadly.

'Oh well, what he lost on the roundabouts, I gained on the swings,' thought Timmy, rather selfishly. At the same time he couldn't help feeling sorry for Odd Bod, but it didn't last long.

That night Odd Bod couldn't get to sleep. He tried reading his book, but this didn't seem to help. The next morning, he woke early. As soon as they had had breakfast, he and Timmy went down to the fair to try to find the man with the china dragon. It was shut. 'Fair opens 6.00 pm' a sign read. Back home, Odd Bod spent another day working hard. The minute six o'clock came, he called Timmy and they made their way to the fair for the second time that day.

'Not again!' thought Timmy. 'Enough's enough, I would have thought. Will he never give up?' This time, the lights were on and everything was working. Odd Bod made straight for the dragon stall. On the way, he bought a sausage for Timmy. As they were getting near the stall, Odd Bod accidentally bumped into a man hurrying away. Under his arm was the china dragon. In his right hand, he was carrying a gold fish in a bowl. Odd Bod was very sad, so sad in fact he was close to tears. The man stopped.

'Excuse me,' he said, 'would you like this gold fish I just won? I have a cat at home and it might eat it.'

'Oh, thank you,' said Odd Bod, brightening immediately. He looked at the fish, twisting about in the bowl. 'Thank you very much indeed. There, Timmy, wasn't that kind?'

'It's all right, I suppose, if you like that sort of thing,' thought the dog. 'It's another mouth to feed, of course, albeit a small one. I'd prefer a bone, myself.' Odd Bod took the bowl and went off towards home. Timmy had his eye on the sausage stand.

'Stick to the main chance and you won't go far wrong,' he was always telling himself, but somehow things seldom seemed to turn out that way. Timmy found, in fact, that the more he calculated, the less successful he seemed to be. However, this did not appear to stop him. He positioned himself close to the stall and sent out his sausage signal. Odd Bod did not get the message.

'This is much better than a rotten old china dragon,' Odd Bod said to Timmy, lifting the gold fish bowl up in the air.

'Is it now?' wondered Timmy, doubtfully. 'What about another sausage?' The dog concentrated especially hard. Once again, however, his powers let him down. 'I can't keep on like this, failing all the time. It's not good for my ego. I shall have to go on a refresher course or something. If I leave it much longer, there won't be much left to refresh.'

Timmy gave one more sniff for luck, without success.

'Fate, I suppose,' he thought, and trotted after Odd Bod. 'It's got a lot to answer for.'

ODD BOD AND THE CHIMNEY SWEEP

Odd Bod was sitting in front of the fire one day. Timmy was, as usual, asleep in his basket. It was very quiet where Odd Bod lived and you really did notice the ticking of the grandfather clock in the hall. Tick, tock, it went. Tick, tock, tick, tock. It used to drive Timmy mad. He barked at it every time it struck. In the end, Odd Bod got so cross with Timmy barking that he stopped it chiming.

Anyway there they were, all nice and quiet, when suddenly a great pile of soot fell down the chimney. Odd Bod jumped out of his rocking chair. 'Good gracious me,' he cried. 'Whatever's that?' Timmy went on sleeping. It would take more than that to wake him. The soot was all over the hearth. 'I will have to get the chimney sweep,' said Odd Bod. 'You won't like that, Timmy, will you?' Odd Bod called to the still sleeping dog. Timmy opened one eye. He heard his name and the word 'sweep'. Not his favourite person, by any means, although he couldn't really think why. 'I'll get him to come tomorrow,' Odd Bod decided.

'Doesn't really matter whether I like it or not. Seems he's coming all the same,' sulked the dog. He could feel very hard done by if he set his mind to it. Odd Bod went to the sweep's house. He was lucky. The man could spare enough time to clean the chimney that day.

'It sounds a bit of an emergency, like,' said the sweep. 'Don't worry though. You've come to the right place. We have a new machine. I think you'll be pleased with her. She's very good. You don't have to cover everything up, because she makes no mess. She's computerised, you see.'

'Hm,' said Odd Bod, guardedly. 'I suppose it's all right, if you say so.' He didn't trust machines. There had been too many times when they had let him down. Understandably, he wasn't at all sure about the latest possible disaster area.

Odd Bod returned home. The sweep arrived two hours later. 'Here we are,' he said to Odd Bod. 'All ready to start.'

'Are we?' Odd Bod replied, rather apprehensively. 'If we must, I suppose we had better. This is the fireplace,' he said, rather stating the obvious.

'Right,' said the sweep. 'Leave me to it.' He had a large black moustache that rather resembled the brush he was about to put up the chimney.

'Come on, Timmy,' said Odd Bod. 'We'll go out into the garden.' Timmy made for his favourite spot, right in a pool of sunlight. Odd Bod decided, on the spur of the moment, to clean the windows. He was just about to fill the bucket from the tap outside the house when there was a great whooshing sound.

Without any warning, an enormous cloud of soot shot out of the chimney and covered everything in sight. Fortunately, Odd Bod did not have his favourite red coat on, but he was wearing his favourite yellow shirt. Instantly it turned a nasty shade of grey. Odd Bod couldn't see through his glasses. They were covered in a thick film of soot.

Timmy wondered about something to eat, but was this the right time for a signal? Wisely, he judged that

it wasn't. Odd Bod seemed very pre-occupied and the signal wouldn't have had a hope of getting through. Timmy transferred his attention to the flowers. 'They're looking a bit down,' he thought. 'Nobody's paying them much attention. I'll give them a quick water.'

He knew that Odd Bod frowned on this particular habit, but Timmy had to get his own back, establish his dominance in some things at least. 'That'll teach you to sit there all day,' he thought. 'Useless things.'

Timmy was not normally malicious, but with flowers he did see red, even when they were daisies. Buttercups were the only ones he quite liked. They were different and had a special sort of quality which he responded to. Maybe it was because they reminded him of his passion – buttered turnips.

Odd Bod shot inside the house. 'Whatever's happening?' he cried to the sweep. The house was in a terrible state. There was soot everywhere. 'Oh dear,' said the sweep. 'I don't know what's gone wrong. The machine's never done that before. She's had a bit of a turn. Instead of sucking she blew, and the soot has gone all over the place.'

'So I see,' said Odd Bod. 'What are we going to do?'

'I'm very sorry,' said the sweep. 'Really I am.'

Just then Timmy came in. Fortunately he had been far enough from the house to have escaped the cloud of soot when it burst through the chimney. 'So much for computers,' thought the dog.

'I wouldn't come in here if I were you,' Odd Bod said. 'Not until I have cleared it up.'

'Nothing like feeling welcome. I mean in your own home. It's coming to something, I'd say.' Timmy returned to the garden. 'Should have left things as they were,' he went on. 'Silly business altogether, really.'

'I don't think there's any more soot in the chimney,' said the sweep.

'One would hope not,' replied Odd Bod. 'It can't be helped, I suppose. I shall just have to clean it up, that's all.'

'Can I give you a hand?' asked the sweep.

'Thank you, I think I can manage,' said Odd Bod, deciding that the man had done enough damage for one day.

'I will have to have her seen to,' said the sweep.

'I think it would be advisable,' said Odd Bod. 'It won't be a very popular service as it is.'

'There's no charge,' volunteered the sweep.

'For what?' enquired Odd Bod.

'My visit.'

'I should hope not.'

'Goodbye, then,' said the sweep, taking up the machine.

'I'll see you out,' said Odd Bod, making sure he had finally got rid of him. 'So much for gadgetry,' he thought. 'It's definitely not what it's cracked up to be.'

Odd Bod heaved a great sigh and fetched in the bucket from outside. He then began the long job of washing everything. The soot was everywhere. It was in all the mugs that were hanging up. It was on the window sills, along the floor, everywhere. Odd Bod worked very hard clearing it all up. When he had finished, the house was sparkling. 'There's a thing,' he said to himself. 'It's made me clean the house right the way through, which I might not have done otherwise.'

Odd Bod was just about to light the fire when another load of soot fell into the fireplace. This time it went all over Odd Bod's face. He choked and coughed. 'Bother the soot,' he said. 'I'm not cleaning that lot up again. It will have to wait until morning. What I need now is a good hot bath. I'll feel better then. But first of all I'll have a cup of tea. Timmy, do you want some milk, boy?'

Timmy was thinking of something rather more substantial, but he wasn't sure what. He was off buttered turnips for the moment. He had thought of them so often, he had sickened himself of them. 'I don't suppose he has any shepherd's pie. No, I shouldn't think so. Pity, I like a good shepherd. Something to get your teeth into, if you see what I mean . . .'

Odd Bod changed his mind and swept up the soot. He drank his tea, lit the fire and had his bath. He sat down in his rocking chair and listened to the grandfather clock. Timmy, quite understandably, fell asleep. It seemed the only thing to do.

'At least nobody can say I had anything to do with it. For once,' he mused, scratching his ear with his front paw as he dozed off. 'Surprising though that may seem.'

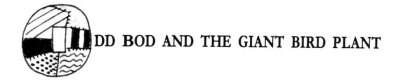

ODD BOD AND THE GIANT BIRD PLANT

Odd Bod woke up one morning and looked out of his window. It was very cold. There was frost on the panes, which made patterns of stars. Odd Bod liked the winter as long as it was dry. Then he didn't mind how cold it was. He liked to see the shape of the trees against a pale orange sky.

Of course, winter wasn't always like that. There were times when Odd Bod longed for the sun, longed to be able to get out into his garden and talk to the tall flowers of summer, the lupins, hollyhocks, foxgloves and of course, his special favourites – roses. This morning, when Odd Bod woke up, the first things he thought about were the birds.

'I must go and get them some wild bird food,' he thought to himself. 'This year there aren't many berries on the trees. The birds are bound to be hungry.'

Odd Bod dressed quickly and went downstairs. Timmy was in his basket. Odd Bod patted him on the head, said 'Good morning, boy' as he always did and put the kettle on to make a cup of tea. 'Here's your milk, Timmy,' he said. 'After breakfast, we must go down to the village and get the birds some food.'

'Never mind the birds, what about me?' thought Timmy. 'Never gives me a thought.' Timmy made short work of the milk. The kettle boiled. Odd Bod made his tea. He also made some porridge and gave some to Timmy.

'Now, boy, we must be off,' he said. 'No time to lose.'

'Must I?' wondered Timmy. 'I suppose so. He'll only start carrying on if I don't.'

Odd Bod and Timmy set off for the village shop. 'Good morning, I'll have a loaf of bread and a packet of wild bird food, please,' Odd Bod said to the lady behind the counter. He paid her, took the things and walked quickly back home. When they reached the cottage, Odd Bod poured some of the bird food into a bowl. Among the nuts, there was one seed that was really huge. 'Goodness, that's a big seed. Look, Timmy!' Odd Bod said, showing the dog the seed. 'I'll save that one and plant it and see whether it will grow.'

'Bound to,' thought Timmy. 'Then what? More flowers of course. One of these days I won't be able to get in the garden for flowers. But at least it will be one seed those stupid birds won't get their beaks on.'

Odd Bod cut up some apples and added some oatmeal. He mixed it with the bird food and added some water to make a special cake. He squeezed the mixture all together. 'There,' he said, 'they'll like that.'

'They're welcome,' mused Timmy. 'As long as there aren't any buttered turnips in it. Which is a point, of course. I must be due for something to eat very soon, surely. No, not while he's so obsessed with those flapping creatures. Wings! I ask you. What good are they? Can you dig a hole with wings? Chew a bone with wings? Will wings lap up milk? They're useless. If they were any good, dogs would have had them long ago. In the natural course of development. About the only thing wings are useful for is flying and what dog of sound mind would want to do that!'

When spring came, Odd Bod took the seed he had

saved and planted it in a pot. He watched and watched and hoped some day he would see a shoot. Odd Bod knew quite a lot about gardens, but he had never seen a seed quite like this one. On the fourteenth day after he had planted it, Odd Bod came downstairs and picked up the pot. There, peeping through the dark brown earth was a tiny green shot. 'It's started, Timmy,' he cried to the rather sleepy dog. Timmy was not very amused at this sudden dancing about. 'Look, boy. The plant is growing.'

Timmy opened one eye. He gave a couple of token wags in order not to upset Odd Bod. 'What a lot of fuss about a silly shoot. He always picks his time too. I was into a very interesting dream about a giant marrow bone and I'd just got to the juicy bit.'

Every day, the plant grew a little more. Odd Bod kept it by the kitchen window. When it was about three inches high, he thought he would plant it in the garden. He put it close to the house where the sun could see it. Sure enough, the plant kept growing. It grew and grew. When it was nearly up to Odd Bod's window, he noticed a bud. 'My bird plant is going to flower. You are a clever plant,' Odd Bod said.

'Funny, talking to a plant,' thought Timmy. 'First signs, I shouldn't wonder, but then I've always had my suspicions . . .'

As the days went by, the bud became larger. One day it began to open out. It was the biggest flower Odd Bod had ever seen. It was the size of a dinner plate. In the centre there was a mass of seeds, and around the seeds were big yellow petals. Odd Bod was delighted. 'Ridiculous,' thought Timmy. 'It must be very insecure if it has to grow that large to prove itself.'

Another week passed by. Odd Bod woke up suddenly one Sunday morning. He went to the window and looked at his bird flower. He couldn't believe his eyes. The plant had gone. It was nowhere to be seen. Odd Bod rushed downstairs, still in his pyjamas.

'Timmy, the bird plant has gone,' Odd Bod yelled to the dog and tore open the back door. There, lying on the ground was the flower. Odd Bod could have cried, it looked so sad. He picked it up and examined the damaged stem. Something had eaten right through it.

Timmy found it difficult to be moved, particularly

out of his basket. Odd Bod fetched a bucket and filled it with water. He put the bird plant in the bucket and hoped that it would live. He felt too sad, even to make himself a cup of tea. He just sat in his rocking chair, wondering how on earth it could have happened. This time it wasn't Timmy's fault. Clearly there was no question of that. He would never have gone that far. Anyway, there were no signs of digging.

'I'm not blaming you, boy,' said Odd Bod.

'I should hope not,' thought Timmy. 'As if I would. As if I'd dare!'

'Not this time, anyway,' continued Odd Bod. 'It must have been those rotten slugs.'

'I'm compared to a slug now, am I?' thought Timmy. 'That's nice, I must say. More likely those beastly birds, I should think. Not that they're much better.'

Then Odd Bod had a really bright thought. 'Never mind,' he said to himself, 'with all those seeds in the flower head, I'll be able to grow lots of bird plants next year. And have plenty of seeds for my bird cake. Maybe things are not so bad, after all.'

'Hm,' thought Timmy. 'Can we really be sure of that? Looks like we're out of milk. Or has he just forgotten. Again.'